A Thorny

Volume 06

CW00520122

Georg Ebers

(Translator: Clara Bell)

Alpha Editions

This edition published in 2023

ISBN : 9789357946032

Design and Setting By
Alpha Editions
www.alphaedis.com
Email - info@alphaedis.com

Contents

VOLUME 6.

CHAPTER XVII.

The philosopher announced the visitor to Caesar, and as some little time elapsed before Melissa came in, Caracalla forgot his theatrical assumption, and sat with a drooping head; for, in consequence, no doubt, of the sunshine which beat on the top of his head, the pain had suddenly become almost unendurably violent.

Without vouchsafing a glance at Melissa, he swallowed one of the alleviating pills left him by Galenus, and hid his face in his hands. The girl came forward, fearless of the lion, for Philostratos had assured her that he was tamed, and most animals were willing to let her touch them. Nor was she afraid of Caesar himself, for she saw that he was in pain, and the alarm with which she had crossed the threshold gave way to pity. Philostratus kept at her side, and anxiously watched Caracalla.

The courage the simple girl showed in the presence of the ferocious brute, and the not less terrible man, struck him favorably, and his hopes rose as a sunbeam fell on her shining hair, which the lady Berenike had arranged with her own hand, twining it with strands of white Bombyx. She must appear, even to this ruthless profligate, as the very type of pure and innocent grace.

Her long robe and peplos, of the finest white wool, also gave her an air of distinction which suited the circumstances. It was a costly garment, which Berenike had had made for Korinna, and she had chosen it from among many instead of the plainer robe in which old Dido had dressed her young mistress. With admirable taste the matron had aimed at giving Melissa a simple, dignified aspect, unadorned and almost priestess-like in its severity. Nothing should suggest the desire to attract, and everything must exclude the idea of a petitioner of the poorer and commoner sort.

Philostratus saw that her appearance had been judiciously cared for; but Caesar's long silence, of which he knew the reason, began to cause him some uneasiness: for, though pain sometimes softened the despot's mood, it more often prompted him to revenge himself, as it were, for his own sufferings, by brutal attacks on the comfort and happiness of others. And, at last, even Melissa seemed to be losing the presence of mind he had admired, for he saw her bosom heave faster and higher, her lips quivered, and her large eyes sparkled through tears.

Caesar's countenance presently cleared a little. He raised his head, and as his eye met Melissa's she pronounced in a low, sweet voice the pleasant Greek greeting, "Rejoice!"

At this moment the philosopher was seized with a panic of anxiety; he felt for the first time the weight of responsibility he had taken on himself. Never had he thought her so lovely, so enchantingly bewitching as now, when she looked up at Caracalla in sweet confusion and timidity, but wholly possessed by her desire to win the favor of the man who, with a word, could make her so happy or so wretched. If this slave of his passions, whom a mere whim perhaps had moved to insist on the strictest morality in his court, should take a fancy to this delightful young creature, she was doomed to ruin. He turned pale, and his heart throbbed painfully as he watched the development of the catastrophe for which he had himself prepared the way.

But, once more, the unexpected upset the philosopher's anticipations. Caracalla gazed at the girl in amazement, utterly discomposed, as though some miracle had happened, or a ghost had started from the ground before him. Springing up, while he clutched the back of his chair, he exclaimed:

"What is this? Do my senses deceive me, or is it some base trickery? No, no! My eyes and my memory are good. This girl—"

"What ails thee, Caesar?" Philostratus broke in, with increasing anxiety.

"Something—something which will silence your foolish doubts—" Caesar panted out. "Patience—wait. Only a minute, and you shall see.—But, first"— and he turned to Melissa—"what is your name, girl?"

"Melissa," she replied, in a low and tremulous voice.

"And your father's and your mother's?"

"Heron is my father's name, and my mother—she is dead—was called Olympias, the daughter of Philip."

"And you are of Macedonian race?"

"Yes, my lord. My father and mother both were of pure Macedonian descent."

The emperor glanced triumphantly at Philostratus, and briefly exclaiming, "That will do, I think," he clapped his hands, and instantly his old chamberlain, Adventus, hurried in from the adjoining room, followed by the whole band of "Caesar's friends." Caracalla, however, only said to them:

"You can wait till I call you.—You, Adventus! I want the gem with the marriage of Alexander." The freedman took the gem out of an ebony casket standing on Caesar's writing-table, and Caracalla, holding the philosopher by the arm, said, with excited emphasis:

"That gem I inherited from my father, the divine Severus. It was engraved before that child came into the world. Now you shall see it, and if you then say that it is an illusion—But why should you doubt it? Pythagoras and your hero Apollonius both knew whose body their souls had inhabited in a former existence. Mine—though my mother has laughed at my belief, and others have dared to do the same-mine, five hundred years ago, dwelt in the greatest of heroes, Alexander the Macedonian—a right royal tabernacle!"

He snatched the gem from the chamberlain's hand, and while he devoured it with his eyes, looking from time to time into Melissa's face, he eagerly ran on:

"It is she. None but a blind man, a fool, a malignant idiot, could doubt it! Any who henceforth shall dare mock at my conviction that I was brought into the world to fulfill the life-span of that great hero, will learn to rue it! Here—it is but natural—here, in the city he founded and which bears his name, I have found positive proof that the bond which unites the son of Philip with the son of Severus is something more than a mere fancy. This maiden—look at her closely—is the re-embodiment of the soul of Roxana, as I am of that of her husband. Even you must see now how naturally it came about that she should uplift her heart and hands in prayer for me. Her soul, when it once dwelt in Roxana, was fondly linked with that of the hero; and now, in the bosom of this simple maiden, it is drawn to the unforgotten fellow-soul which has found its home in my breast."

He spoke with enthusiastic and firm conviction of the truth of his strange imagining, as though he were delivering a revelation from the gods. He bade Philostratus approach and compare the features of Roxana, as carved in the onyx, with those of the young supplicant.

The fair Persian stood facing Alexander; they were clasping each other's hands in pledge of marriage, and a winged Hymen fluttered above their heads with his flaming torch.

Philostratus was, in fact, startled as he looked at the gem, and expressed his surprise in the liveliest terms, for the features of Roxana as carved in the cameo, no larger than a man's palm, were, line for line, those of the daughter of Heron. And this sport of chance could not but be amazing to any one who did not know—as neither of the three who were examining the gem knew— that it was a work of Heron's youth, and that he had given Roxana the features of his bride Olympias, whose living image her daughter Melissa had grown to be.

"And how long have you had this work of art?" asked Philostratus.

"I inherited it, as I tell you, from my father," replied Caracalla. "Severus sometimes wore it.—But wait. After the battle of Issos, in his triumph over Pescennius Niger—I can see him now—he wore it on his shoulder, and that was—"

"Two-and-twenty years ago," the philosopher put in; and Caracalla, turning to Melissa, asked her:

"How old are you, child?"

"Eighteen, my lord." And the reply delighted Caesar; he laughed aloud, and looked triumphantly at Philostratus.

The philosopher willingly admitted that there was something strange in the incident, and he congratulated Caesar on having met with such strong confirmation of his inward conviction. The soul of Alexander might now do great things through him.

During this conversation the alarm which had come over Melissa at Caesar's silence had entirely disappeared. The despot whose suffering had appealed to her sympathetic soul, now struck her as singular rather than terrible. The idea that she, the humble artist's daughter, could harbor the soul of a Persian princess, amused her; and when the lion lifted his head and lashed the floor with his tail at her approach, she felt that she had won his approbation. Moved by a sudden impulse, she laid her hand on his head and boldly stroked it. The light, warm touch soothed the fettered prince of the desert, and, rubbing his brow against Melissa's round arm, he muttered a low, contented growl.

At this Caesar was enchanted; it was to him a further proof of his strange fancy. The "Sword of Persia" was rarely so friendly to any one; and Theocritus owed much of the favor shown him by Caracalla to the fact that at their first meeting the lion had been on particularly good terms with him. Still, the brute had never shown so much liking for any stranger as for this young girl, and never responded with such eager swinging of his tail excepting to Caesar's own endearments. It must be instinct which had revealed to the beast the old and singular bond which linked his master and this new acquaintance. Caracalla, who, in all that happened to him, traced the hand of a superior power, pointed this out to Philostratus, and asked him whether, perhaps, the attack of pain he had just suffered might not have yielded so quickly to the presence of the revived Roxana rather than to Galen's pills.

Philostratus thought it wise not to dispute this assumption, and soon diverted the conversation to the subject of Melissa's imprisoned relations. He quietly represented to Caracalla that his noblest task must be to satisfy the spirit of her who had been so dear to the hero whose life he was to fulfill; and Caesar, who was delighted that the philosopher should recognize as a fact the illusion which flattered him, at once agreed. He questioned Melissa about her brother Alexander with a gentleness of which few would have thought him capable; and the sound of her voice, as she answered him modestly but frankly and with sisterly affection, pleased him so well that he allowed her to speak without interruption longer than was his wont. Finally, he promised her that he would question the painter, and, if possible, be gracious to him.

He again clapped his hands, and ordered a freedman named Epagathos, who was one of his favorite body-servants, to send immediately for Alexander from the prison.

As before, when Adventus had been summoned, a crowd followed Epagathos, and, as Caesar did not dismiss them, Melissa was about to withdraw; the despot, however, desired her to wait.

Blushing, and confused with shyness, she remained standing by Caesar's seat; and though she only ventured to raise her eyes now and then for a stolen look, she felt herself the object of a hundred curious, defiant, bold, or contemptuous glances.

How gladly would she have escaped, or have sunk into the earth! But there she had to stand, her teeth set, while her lips trembled, to check the tears which would rise.

Caesar, meanwhile, took no further notice of her. He was longing to relate at full length, to his friends and companions, the wonderful and important thing that had happened; but he would not approach the subject while they took their places in his presence. Foremost of them, with Theocritus, came the high-priest of Serapis, and Caracalla immediately desired them to introduce the newly appointed head-guardian of the peace. But the election was not yet final. The choice lay, Theocritus explained, between two equally good men. One, Aristides, was a Greek of high repute, and the other was only an Egyptian, but so distinguished for zealous severity that, for his part, he should vote for him.

At this the high-priest broke in, saying that the man favored by Theocritus did in fact possess the qualities for which he was commended, but in such a measure that he was utterly hated by the Greek population; and in Alexandria more could be achieved by justice and mercy than by defiant severity.

But at this the favorite laughed, and said that he was convinced of the contrary. A populace which could dare to mock at the divine Caesar, the guest of their city, with such gross audacity, must be made to smart under the power of Rome and its ruler. The deposed magistrate had lost his place for the absurd measures he had proposed, and Aristides was in danger of following in his footsteps.

"By no means," the high-priest said, with calm dignity. "The Greek, whom I would propose, is a worthy and determined man. Now, Zminis the Egyptian, the right hand of the man who has been turned out, is, it must be said, a wretch without ruth or conscience."

But here the discussion was interrupted. Melissa, whose ears had tingled as she listened, had started with horror as she heard that Zminis, the in former, was to be appointed to the command of the whole watch of the city. If this should happen, her brothers and father were certainly lost. This must be prevented. As the high-priest ceased speaking, she laid her hand on Caesar's, and, when he looked up at her in surprise, she whispered to him, so low and so quickly that hardly any one observed it "Not Zminis; he is our mortal enemy!"

Caracalla scarcely glanced at the face of the daring girl, but he saw how pale she had turned. The delicate color in her cheeks, and the dimple he had seen while she stroked the lion had struck him as particularly fascinating. This had helped to make her so like the Roxana on the gem, and the change in her roused his pity. She must smile again; and so, accustomed as he was to visit his annoyance on others, he angrily exclaimed to his "Friends":

"Can I be everywhere at once? Can not the simplest matter be settled without me? It was the praetorian prefect's business to report to me concerning the two candidates, if you could not agree; but I have not seen him since last evening. The man who has to be sought when I need him neglects his duty! Macrinus usually knows his. Does any one know what has detained him?"

The question was asked in an angry, nay, in an ominous tone, but the praetorian prefect was a powerful personage, whose importance made him almost invulnerable. Yet the praetor Lucius Priscillianus was ready with an answer. He was the most malicious and ill-natured scandal-monger at court; and he hated the prefect, for he himself had coveted the post, which was the highest in the state next to Caesar's. He had always some slaves set to spy upon Macrinus, and he now said, with a contemptuous shrug:

"It is a marvel to me that so zealous a man—though he is already beginning to break down under his heavy duties—should be so late. However, he here spends his evenings and nights in special occupations, which must of course be far from beneficial to the health and peace of mind which his office demands."

"What can those be?" asked Caracalla; but the praetor added without a pause:

"Merciful gods! Who would not crave to glance into the future?"

"And it is that which makes him late?" said Caesar, with more curiosity than anger.

"Hardly by broad daylight," replied Priscillianus. "The spirits he would fain evoke shun the light of day, it is said. But he may be weary with late watching and painful agitations."

"Then he calls up spirits at night?"

"Undoubtedly, great Caesar. But, in this capital of philosophy, spirits are illogical it would seem. How can Macrinus interpret the prophecy that he, who is already on the highest step attainable to us lower mortals, shall rise yet higher?"

"We will ask him," said Caesar, indifferently. "But you—guard your tongue. It has already cost some men their heads, whom I would gladly see yet among the living. Wishes can not be punished. Who does not wish to stand on the step next above his own? You, my friend, would like that of Macrinus.—But deeds! You know me! I am safe from them, so long as each of you so sincerely grudges his neighbor every promotion. You, my Lucius, have again proved how keen your sight is, and, if it were not too great an honor for this refractory city to have a Roman in the toga praetexta at the head of its administration, I should like to make you the guardian of the peace here. You see me," he went on, "in an elated mood to-day.—Cilo, you know this gem which came to me from my father. Look at it, and at this maiden.—Come nearer, priest of the divine Alexander; and you too consider the marvel, Theocritus, Antigonus, Dio, Pandion, Paulinus. Compare the face of the female figure with this girl by my side. The master carved this Roxana long before she was born. You are surprised? As Alexander's soul dwells in me, so she is Roxana, restored to life. It has been proved by irrefragable evidence in the presence of Philostratus."

The priest of Alexander here exclaimed, in a tone of firm conviction:

"A marvel indeed! We bow down to the noble vessel of the soul of Alexander. I, the priest of that hero, attest that great Caesar has found that in which Roxana's soul now exists." And as he spoke he pressed his hand to his heart, bowing low before Caesar; the rest imitated his example. Even Julius Paulinus, the satirist, followed the Roman priest's lead; but he whispered in the ear of Cassius Dio "Alexander's soul was inquisitive, and wanted to see how it could live in the body which, of all mortal tenements on earth, least resembles his own."

A mocking word was on the ex-consul's lips as to the amiable frame of mind which had so suddenly come over Caesar; but he preferred to watch and listen, as Caracalla beckoned Theocritus to him and begged him to give up the appointment of Zminis, though, as a rule, he indulged the favorite's every whim. He could not bear, he said, to intrust the defense of his own person and of the city of Alexander to an Egyptian, so long as a Greek could be found capable of the duty. He proposed presently to have the two candidates brought before him, and to decide between them in the presence of the prefect of the praetorians. Then, turning to those of his captains who stood around him, he said:

"Greet my soldiers from me. I could not show myself to them yesterday. I saw just now, with deep regret, how the rain has drenched them in this luxurious city. I will no longer endure it. The praetorians and the Macedonian legion shall be housed in quarters of which they will tell wonders for a long time to come. I would rather see them sleeping in white wool and eating off silver than these vile traders. Tell them that."

He was here interrupted, for Epagathos announced a deputation from the Museum, and, at the same time, the painter Alexander, who had been brought from prison. At this Caracalla exclaimed with disgust:

"Spare me the hair-splitting logicians!—Do you, Philostratus, receive them in my name. If they make any impudent demands, you may tell them my opinion of them and their Museum. Go, but come back quickly. Bring in the painter. I will speak with him alone.—You, my friends, withdraw with our idiologos, the priest of Alexander, who is well known here, and visit the city. I shall not require you at present."

The whole troop hastened to obey. Caracalla now turned to Melissa once more, and his eye brightened as he again discerned the dimple in her cheeks, which had recovered their roses. Her imploring eyes met his, and the happy expectation of seeing her brother lent them a light which brought joy to the friendless sovereign. During his last speech he had looked at her from time to time; but in the presence of so many strangers she had avoided meeting his gaze. Now she thought that she might freely show him that his favor was a happiness to her. Her soul, as Roxana, must of course feel drawn to his; in that he firmly believed. Her prayer and sacrifice for him sufficiently proved it—as he told himself once more.

When Alexander was brought in, it did not anger him to see that the brother, who held out his arms to Melissa in his habitual eager way, had to be reminded by her of the imperial presence. Every homage was due to this fair being, and he was, besides, much struck by Alexander's splendid appearance. It was long since any youthful figure had so vividly reminded him of the marble statues of the great Athenian masters. Melissa's brother stood before him, the very embodiment of the ideal of Greek strength and manly beauty. His mantle had been taken from him in prison, and he wore only the short chiton, which also left bare his powerful but softly modeled arms. He had been allowed no time to arrange and anoint his hair, and the light-brown curls were tossed in disorderly abundance about his shapely head. This favorite of the gods appeared in Caesar's eyes as an Olympic victor, who had come to claim the wreath with all the traces of the struggle upon him.

No sign of fear, either of Caesar or his lion, marred this impression. His bow, as he approached the potentate, was neither abject nor awkward, and Caesar felt bitter wrath at the thought that this splendid youth, of all men, should have selected him as the butt of his irony. He would have regarded it as a peculiar gift of fortune if this man—such a brother of such a sister—could but love him, and, with the eye of an artist, discern in the despot the great qualities which, in spite of his many crimes, he believed he could detect in himself. And he hoped, with an admixture of anxiety such as he had never known before, that the painter's demeanor would be such as should allow him to show mercy.

When Alexander besought him with a trustful mien to consider his youth, and the Alexandrian manners which he had inherited both from his parents and his grandparents, if indeed his tongue had wagged too boldly in speaking of the all-powerful Caesar, and to remember the fable of the lion and the mouse, the scowl he had put on to impress the youth with his awfulness and power vanished from Caesar's brow. The idea that this great artist, whose sharp eye could so surely distinguish the hideous from the beautiful, should regard him as ill-favored, was odious to him. He had listened to him in silence; but suddenly he inquired of Alexander whether it was indeed he, whom he had never injured, who had written the horrible epigram nailed with the rope to the door of the Serapeum and when the painter emphatically denied it, Caesar breathed as though a burden had fallen from his soul. He nevertheless insisted on hearing from the youth's own lips what it was that he had actually dared to say. After some hesitation, during which Melissa besought Caesar in vain to spare her and her brother this confession, Alexander exclaimed:

"Then the hunted creature must walk into the net, and, unless your clemency interferes, on to death! What I said referred partly to the wonderful strength that you, my lord, have so often displayed in the field and in the circus; and also to another thing, which I myself now truly repent of having alluded to. It is said that my lord killed his brother."

"That—ah! that was it!" said Caesar, and his face, involuntarily this time, grew dark.

"Yes, my lord," Alexander went on, breathing hard. "To deny it would be to add a second crime to the former one, and I am one of those who would rather jump into cold water both feet at once, when it has to be done. All the world knows what your strength is; and I said that it was greater than that of Father Zeus; for that he had cast his son Hephaestos only on the earth, and your strong fist had cast your brother through the earth into the depths of Hades. That was all. I have not added nor concealed anything."

Melissa had listened in terror to this bold confession. Papinian, the brave praetorian prefect, one of the most learned lawyers of his time, had incurred Caracalla's fury by refusing to say that the murder of Geta was not without excuse; and his noble answer, that it was easier to commit fratricide than to defend it, cost him his life.

So long as Caesar had been kind to her, Melissa had felt repelled by him; but now, when he was angry, she was once more attracted to him.

As the wounds of a murdered man are said to bleed afresh when the murderer approaches, Caracalla's irritable soul was wont to break out in a frenzy of rage when any one was so rash as to allude to this, his foulest crime. This reference to his brother's death had as usual stirred his wrath, but he controlled it; for as a torrent of rain extinguishes the fire which a lightning-flash has kindled, the homage to his strength, in Alexander's satire, had modified his indignation. The irony which made the artist's contemptuous words truly witty, would not have escaped Caracalla's notice if they had applied to any one else; but he either did not feel it, or would not remark it, for the sake of leaving Melissa in the belief that his physical strength was really wonderful. Besides, he thus could indulge his wish to avoid pronouncing sentence of death on this youth; he only measured him with a severe eye, and said in threatening tones, to repay mockery in kind and to remind the criminal of the fate imperial clemency should spare him:

"I might be tempted to try my strength on you, but that it is worse to try a fall with a vaporing wag, the sport of the winds, than with the son of Caesar. And if I do not condescend to the struggle, it is because you are too light for such an arm as this." And as he spoke he boastfully grasped the muscles which constant practice had made thick and firm. "But my hand reaches far. Every man-at-arms is one of its fingers, and there are thousands of them. You have made acquaintance already, I fancy, with those which clutched you."

"Not so," replied Alexander, with a faint smile, as he bowed humbly. "I should not dare resist your great strength, but the watch-dogs of the law tried in vain to track me. I gave myself up."

"Of your own accord?"

"To procure my father's release, as he had been put in prison."

"Most magnanimous!" said Caesar, ironically. "Such a deed sounds well, but is apt to cost a man his life. You seem to have overlooked that. "No, great Caesar; I expected to die."

"Then you are a philosopher, a contemner of life."

"Neither. I value life above all else; for, if it is taken from me, there is an end of enjoying its best gifts."

"Best gifts!" echoed Caesar. "I should like to know which you honor with the epithet."

"Love and art."

"Indeed?" said Caracalla, with a swift glance at Melissa. Then, in an altered voice, he added, "And revenge?"

"That," said the artist, boldly, "is a pleasure I have not yet tasted. No one ever did me a real injury till the villain Zminis robbed my guiltless father of his liberty; and he is not worthy to do such mischief, as a finger of your imperial hand."

At this, Caesar looked at him suspiciously, and said in stern tones:

"But you have now the opportunity of trying the fine flavor of vengeance. If I were timid—since the Egyptian acted only as my instrument—I should have cause to protect myself against you."

"By no means," said the painter, with an engaging smile, "it lies in your power to do me the greatest benefit. Do it, Caesar! It would be a joy to me to show that, though I have been reckless beyond measure, I am nevertheless a grateful man."

"Grateful?" repeated Caracalla, with a cruel laugh. Then he rose slowly, and looked keenly at Alexander, exclaiming:

"I should almost like to try you."

"And I will answer for it that you will never regret it!" Melissa put in. "Greatly as he has erred, he is worthy of your clemency."

"Is he?" said Caesar, looking down at her kindly. "What Roxana's soul affirms by those rosy lips I can not but believe."

Then again he paused, studying Alexander with a searching eye, and added:

"You think me strong; but you will change that opinion—which I value— if I forgive you like a poor-spirited girl. You are in my power. You risked your life. If I give it you, I must have a gift in return, that I may not be cheated."

"Set my father free, and he will do whatever you may require of him," Melissa broke out. But Caracalla stopped her, saying: "No one makes conditions with Caesar. Stand back, girl."

Melissa hung her head and obeyed; but she stood watching the eager discussion between these two dissimilar men, at first with anxiety and then with surprise.

Alexander seemed to resist Caesar's demands; but presently the despot must have proposed something which pleased the artist, for Melissa heard the low, musical laugh which had often cheered her in moments of sadness. Then the conversation was more serious, and Caracalla said, so loud that Melissa could hear him:

"Do not forget to whom you speak. If my word is not enough, you can go back to prison." Then again she trembled for her brother; but some soft word of his mollified the fury of the terrible man, who was never the same for two minutes together. The lion, too, which lay unchained by his master's seat, gave her a fright now and then; for if Caesar raised his voice in anger, he growled and stood up.

How fearful were this beast and his lord! Rather would she spend her whole life on a ship's deck, tossed to and fro by the surges, than share this man's fate. And yet there was in him something which attracted her; nay, and it nettled her that he should forget her presence.

At last Alexander humbly asked Caracalla whether he might not tell Melissa to what he had pledged his word.

"That shall be my business," replied Caesar. "You think that a mere girl is a better witness than none at all. Perhaps you are right. Then let it be understood: whatever you may have to report to me, my wrath shall not turn against you. This fellow—why should you not be told, child?— is going into the town to collect all the jests and witty epigrams which have been uttered in my honor."

"Alexander!" cried Melissa, clasping her hands and turning pale with horror. But Caracalla laughed to himself, and went on cheerfully:

"Yes, it is dangerous work, no doubt; and for that reason I pledged my word as Caesar not to require him to pay for the sins of others. On the contrary, he is free, if the posy he culls for me is sufficient."

"Ay," said Alexander, on whom his sister's white face and warning looks were having effect. "But you made me another promise on which I lay great stress. You will not compel me to tell you, nor try to discover through any other man, who may have spoken or written any particular satire."

"Enough!" said Caracalla, impatiently; but Alexander was not to be checked. He went on vehemently: "I have not forgotten that you said conditions were not to be made with Caesar; but, in spite of my impotence, I maintain the right of returning to my prison and there awaiting my doom, unless you once more assure me, in this girl's presence, that you will neither inquire as to the names of the authors of any gibes I may happen to have heard, nor compel me by any means whatever to give up the names of the writers of epigrams. Why should I not satisfy your curiosity and your relish of a sharp jest? But rather than do the smallest thing which might savor of treachery—ten times rather the axe or the gallows!"

And Caracalla replied with a dark frown, loudly and briefly:

"I promise."

"And if your rage is too much for you?" wailed Melissa, raising her hands in entreaty; but the despot replied, sternly:

"There is no passion which can betray Caesar into perjury."

At this moment Philostratus came in again, with Epagathos, who announced the praetorian prefect. Melissa, encouraged by the presence of her kind protector, went on:

But, great Caesar, you will release my father and my other brother?"

"Perhaps," replied Caracalla. "First we will see how this one carries out his task."

"You will be satisfied, my lord," said the young man, looking quite happy again, for he was delighted at the prospect of saying audacious things to the face of the tyrant whom all were bent on flattering, and holding up the mirror to him without, as he firmly believed, bringing any danger on himself or others.

He bowed to go. Melissa did the same, saying, as airily as though she were free to come and go here:

"Accept my thanks, great Caesar. Oh, how fervently will I pray for you all my life, if only you show mercy to my father and brothers!"

"That means that you are leaving me?" asked Caracalla.

"How can it be otherwise?" said Melissa, timidly. "I am but a girl, and the men whom you expect—"

"But when they are gone?" Caesar insisted.

"Even then you can not want me," she murmured.

"You mean," said Caracalla, bitterly, "that you are afraid to come back. You mean that you would rather keep out of the way of the man you prayed for, so long as he is well. And if the pain which first aroused your sympathy attacks him again, even then will you leave the irascible sovereign to himself or the care of the gods?"

"Not so, not so," said Melissa, humbly, looking into his eyes with an expression that pierced him to the heart, so that he added, with gentle entreaty:

"Then show that you are she whom I believe you to be. I do not compel you. Go whither you will, stay away even if I send for you; but"—and here his brow clouded again—"why should I try to be merciful to her from whom I looked for sympathy and kindliness, when she flees from me like the rest?"

"O my lord!" Melissa sighed distressfully. "Go!" Caesar went on. "I do not need you."

"No, no," the girl cried, in great trouble. "Call me, and I will come. Only shelter me from the others, and from their looks of scorn; only— O immortal gods!—If you need me, I will serve you, and willingly, with all my heart. But if you really care for me, if you desire my presence, why let me suffer the worst?" Here a sudden flood of tears choked her utterance. A smile of triumph passed over Caesar's features, and drawing Melissa's hands away from her tearful face, he said, kindly:

"Alexander's soul pines for Roxana's; that is what makes your presence so dear to me. Never shall you have cause to rue coming at my call. I swear it by the manes of my divine father—you, Philostratus, are witness."

The philosopher, who thought he knew Caracalla, gave a sigh of relief; and Alexander gladly reflected that the danger he had feared for his sister was averted. This craze about Roxana, of which Caracalla had just now spoken to him as a certain fact, he regarded as a monstrous illusion of this strange man's, which would, however, be a better safeguard for Melissa than pledges and oaths.

He clasped her hand, and said with cheerful confidence: "Only send for her when you are ill, my lord, as long as you remain here. I know from your own lips that there is no passion which can betray Caesar into perjury. Will you permit her to come with me for the present?"

"No," said Caracalla, sharply, and he bade him go about the business he had in hand. Then, turning to Philostratus, he begged him to conduct Melissa to Euryale, the high-priest's noble wife, for she had been a kind and never-forgotten friend of his mother's.

The philosopher gladly escorted the young girl to the matron, who had long been anxiously awaiting her return.

CHAPTER XVIII.

The statue of Serapis, a figure of colossal size, carved by the master-hand of Bryaxis, out of ivory overlaid with gold, sat enthroned in the inner chamber of the great Temple of Serapis, with the kalathos crowning his bearded face, and the three-headed Cerberus at his feet, gazing down in supreme silence on the scene around. He did not lack for pious votaries and enthusiastic admirers, for, so long as Caesar was his guest, the curtain was withdrawn which usually hid his majestic form from their eyes. But his most devoted worshipers thought that the god's noble, benevolent, grave countenance had a wrathful look; for, though nothing had been altered in this, the finest pillared hall in the world; though the beautiful pictures in relief on the walls and ceiling, the statues and altars of marble, bronze, and precious metals between the columns, and the costly mosaic-work of many colors which decked the floor in regular patterns, were the same as of yore, this splendid pavement was trodden to-day by thousands of feet which had no concern with the service of the god.

Before Caesar's visit, solemn silence had ever reigned in this worthy home of the deity, fragrant with the scarcely visible fumes of kyphi; and the worshipers gathered without a sound round the foot of his statue, and before the numerous altars and the smaller images of the divinities allied to him or the votive tablets recording the gifts and services instituted in honor of Serapis by pious kings or citizens. On feast-days, and during daily worship, the chant of priestly choirs might be heard, or the murmur of prayer; and the eye might watch the stolists who crowned the statues with flowers and ribbons, as required by the ritual, or the processions of priests in their various rank. Carrying sacred relics and figures of the gods on trays or boats, with emblematic standards, scepters, and cymbals, they moved about the sacred precinct in prescribed order, and most of them fulfilled their duties with devotion and edification.

But Caesar's presence seemed to have banished these solemn feelings. From morning till night the great temple swarmed with visitors, but their appearance and demeanor were more befitting the market-place or public bath than the sanctuary. It was now no more than the anteroom to Caesar's audience-chamber, and thronged with Roman senators, legates, tribunes, and other men of rank, and the clients and "friends" of Caesar, mingled with soldiers of inferior grades, scribes, freedmen, and slaves, who had followed in Caracalla's train. There were, too, many Alexandrians who expected to gain some benefit, promotion, or distinction through the emperor's favorites. Most of these kept close to his friends and intimates, to make what profit they could out of them. Some were corn and wine dealers, or armorers, who wished to obtain contracts for supplying the army; others were usurers, who had money to lend on the costly objects which warriors often acquired as booty; and here, as everywhere, bedizened and painted women were crowding round the free- handed strangers. There were Magians, astrologers, and magicians by the dozen, who considered this sacred spot the most suitable place in which to offer their services to the Romans, always inquisitive for signs and charms. They knew how highly Egyptian magic was esteemed throughout the empire; though their arts were in fact prohibited, each outdid the other in urgency, and not less in a style of dress which should excite curiosity and expectancy.

Serapion held aloof. Excepting that he wore a beard and robe, his appearance even had nothing in common with them; and his talar was not like theirs, embroidered with hieroglyphics, tongues, and flames, but of plain white stuff, which gave him the aspect of a learned and priestly sage.

As Alexander, on his way through the temple to fulfill Caesar's commission, went past the Magian, Castor, his supple accomplice, stole up behind a statue, and, when the artist disappeared in the crowd, whispered to his master:

"The rascally painter is at liberty!"

"Till further notice!" was the reply, and Serapion was about to give his satellite some instructions, when a hand was laid on his shoulder, and Zminis said in a low voice:

"I am glad to have found you here. Accusations are multiplying against you, my friend; and though I have kept my eyes shut till now, that cannot last much longer."

"Let us hope you are mistaken," replied the Magian, firmly. And then he went on in a hurried whisper: "I know what your ambition is, and my support may be of use to you. But we must not be seen together. We will meet again in the instrument-room, to the left of the first stairs up to the observatory. You will find me there."

"At once, then," said the other. "I am to be in Caesar's presence in a quarter of an hour."

The Magian, as being one of the most skillful makers of astronomical instruments, and attached to the sanctuary, had a key of the room he had designated. Zminis found him there, and their business was quickly settled. They knew each other well, and each knew things of the other which inspired them with mutual fear. However, as time pressed, they set aside all useless antagonisms, to unite against the common foe.

The Magian knew already that Zminis had been named to Caesar as a possible successor to the chief of the night-watch, and that he had a powerful rival. By the help of the Syrian, whose ventriloquism was so perfect that he never failed to produce the illusion that his feigned voice proceeded from any desired person or thing, Serapion had enmeshed the praetorian prefect, the greatest magnate in the empire next to Caesar himself, and in the course of the past night had gained a firm hold over him.

Macrinus, a man of humble birth, who owed his promotion to Severus, the father of Caracalla, had, the day before, been praying in the Pantheon to the statue of his deceased patron. A voice had proceeded from the image, telling him that the divine Severus needed him for a great work. A pious seer was charged to tell him more exactly what this was; and he would meet him if he went at about sunset to the shrine of Isis, and called three times on the name of Severus before the altar of the goddess.

The Syrian ventriloquist had, by Serapion's orders, hidden behind a pillar and spoken to the prefect from the statue; and Macrinus had, of course, obeyed his instructions. He had met the Magian in the Temple of Isis, and what he had seen, heard, and felt during the night had so deeply affected him that he had promised to revisit Serapion the next evening. What means he had used to enslave so powerful a man the Magian did not tell his ally; but he declared that Macrinus was as wax in his hands, and he came to an agreement with the Egyptian that if he, Serapion, should bring about the promotion for which Zminis sighed, Zminis, on his part, should give him a free hand, and commend his arts to Caesar.

It needed but a few minutes to conclude this compact; but then the Magian proceeded to insist that Alexander's father and brother should be made away with.

"Impossible," replied Zminis. "I should be only too glad to wring the necks of the whole brood; but, as it is, I am represented to Caesar as too stern and ruthless. And a pretty little slut, old Heron's daughter, has entangled him in her toils."

"No," said Serapion, positively. "I have seen the girl, and she is as innocent as a child. But I know the force of contrast: when depravity meets purity—"

"Come, no philosophizing!" interrupted the other. "We have better things to attend to, and one or the other may turn to your advantage."

And he told him that Caesar, whose whim it was to spare Alexander's life, regarded Melissa as an incarnation of Roxana.

"That is worth considering," said the Magian, stroking his beard meditatively; then he suddenly exclaimed:

"By the law, as you know, all the relatives of a state criminal are sent to the quarries or the mines. Dispatch Heron and his philosopher son forthwith.

Whither?—that is your concern; only, for the next few days they must be out of reach."

"Good!" said the Egyptian, and an odious smile overspread his thin brown face. "They may go as galley-slaves and row themselves to the Sardinian mines. A good idea!"

"I have even better ideas than that to serve a friend," replied Serapion. "Only get the philosopher out of the way. If Caesar lends an ear to his ready tongue, I shall never see you guardian of the peace. The painter is less dangerous."

"He shall share their fate," cried the spy, and he licked his thick lips as if tasting some dainty morsel. He waved an adieu to the Magian, and hastened back to the great hall. There he strictly instructed one of his subordinates to take care that the gem-cutter and his son Philip found places on board a galley bound for Sardinia.

At the great door he again met Serapion, with the Syrian at his heels, and the Magian said:

"My friend here has just seen a clay figure, molded by some practiced hand. It represents Caesar as a defiant warrior, but in the shape of a deformed dwarf. It is hideously like him; you can see it at the Elephant tavern."

The Egyptian pressed his hand, with an eager "That will serve," and hastily went out.

Two hours slipped by, and Zminis was still waiting in Caesar's anteroom. The Greek, Aristides, shared his fate, the captain hitherto of the armed guard; while Zminis had been the head of the spies, intrusted with communicating written reports to the chief of the night-watch. The Greek's noble, soldierly figure looked strikingly fine by the slovenly, lank frame of the tall Egyptian. They both knew that within an hour or so one would be supreme over the other; but of this they thought it best to say nothing. Zminis, as was his custom when he wished to assume an appearance of respect which he did not feel, was alternately abject and pressingly confidential; while Aristides calmly accepted his hypocritical servility, and answered it with dignified condescension. Nor had they any lack of subjects, for their interests were the same, and they both had the satisfaction of reflecting what injury must ensue to public safety through their long and useless detention here.

But when two full hours had elapsed without their being bidden to Caesar's presence, or taken any notice of by their supporters, Zminis grew wroth, and the Greek frowned in displeasure. Meanwhile the anteroom was every moment more crowded, and neither chose to give vent to his anger. Still, when the door to the inner chambers was opened for a moment, and loud laughter and the ring of wine-cups fell on their ears, Aristides shrugged his shoulders, and the Egyptian's eyes showed an ominous white ring glaring out of his brown face.

Caracalla had meanwhile received the praetorian prefect; he had forgiven him his long delay, when Macrinus, of his own accord, had told him of the wonderful things Serapion had made known to him. The prefect's son, too, had been invited to the banquet of Seleukus; and when Caracalla heard from him and others of the splendor of the feast, he had begun to feel hungry. Even with regard to food, Caesar acted only on the impulse of the moment; and though, in the field, he would, to please his soldiers, be content with a morsel of bread and a little porridge, at home he highly appreciated the pleasures of the table. Whenever he gave the word, an abundant meal must at once be ready. It was all the same to him what was kept waiting or postponed, so long as something to his taste was set before him. Macrinus, indeed, humbly reminded him that the guardians of the peace were awaiting him; but he only waved his hand with contempt, and proceeded to the dining-room, which was soon filled with a large number of guests. Within a few minutes the first dish was set before his couch, and, as plenty of good stories were told, and an admirable band of flute-playing and singing girls filled up the pauses in the conversation, he enjoyed his meal. In spite, too, of the warning which Galenus had impressed on his Roman physician, he drank freely of the fine wine which had been brought out for him from the airy lofts of the Serapeum, and those about him were surprised at their master's unwonted good spirits.

He was especially gracious to the high-priest, whom he bade to a place by his side; and he even accepted his arm as a support, when, the meal being over, they returned to the tablinum.

'There he flung himself on a couch, with a burning head, and began feeding the lion, without paying any heed to his company. It was a pleasure to him to see the huge brute rend a young lamb. When the remains of this introductory morsel had been removed and the pavement washed, he gave the "Sword of Persia" pieces of raw flesh, teasing the beast by snatching the daintiest bits out of his mouth, and then offering them to him again, till the satiated brute stretched himself yawning at his feet. During this entertainment, he had a letter read to him from the senate, and dictated a reply to a secretary. His eyes twinkled with a tipsy leer in his flushed face, and yet he was perfectly competent; and his instructions to the senate, though imperious indeed, were neither more nor less rational than in his soberest moods.

Then, after washing his hands in a golden basin, he acted on Macrinus's suggestion, and the two candidates who had so long been waiting were at last admitted. The prefect of the praetorians had, by the Magian's desire, recommended the Egyptian; but Caesar wished to see for himself, and then to decide. Both the applicants had received hints from their supporters: the Egyptian, to moderate his rigor; the Greek, to express himself in the severest terms. And this was made easy for him, for the annoyance which had been pent up during his three hours' waiting was sufficient to lend his handsome face a stern look. Zminis strove to appear mild by assuming servile humility; but this so ill became his cunning features that Caracalla saw with secret satisfaction that he could accede to Melissa's wishes, and confirm the choice of the high- priest, in whose god he had placed his hopes.

Still, his own safety was more precious to him than the wishes of any living mortal; so he began by pouring out, on both, the vials of his wrath at the bad management of the town. Their blundering tools had not even succeeded in capturing the most guileless of men, the painter Alexander. The report that the men-at-arms had seized him had been a fabrication to deceive, for the artist had given himself up. Nor had he as yet heard of any other traitor whom they had succeeded in laying hands on, though the town was flooded with insolent epigrams directed against the imperial person. And, as he spoke, he glared with fury at the two candidates before him.

The Greek bowed his head in silence, as if conscious of his short- comings; the Egyptian's eyes flashed, and, with an amazingly low bend of his supple spine, he announced that, more than three hours since, he had discovered a most abominable caricature in clay, representing Caesar as a soldier in a horrible pygmy form.

"And the perpetrator," snarled Caracalla, listening with a scowl for the reply.

Zminis explained that great Caesar himself had commanded his attendance just as he hoped to find the traces of the criminal, and that, while he was waiting, more than three precious hours had been lost. At this Caracalla broke out in a fury:

"Catch the villain! And let me see his insolent rubbish. Where are your eyes? You bungling louts ought to protect me against the foul brood that peoples this city, and their venomous jests. Past grievances are forgotten. Set the painter's father and brother at liberty. They have had a warning. Now I want something new. Something new, I say; and, above all, let me see the ringleaders in chains; the man who nailed up the rope, and the caricaturists. We must have them, to serve as an example to the others."

Aristides thought that the moment had now come for displaying his severity, and he respectfully but decidedly represented to Caesar that he would advise that the gem-cutter and his son should be kept in custody. They were well-known persons, and too great clemency would only aggravate the virulence of audacious tongues. The painter was free, and if his relatives were also let out of prison, there was nothing to prevent their going off to the other end of the world. Alexandria was a seaport, and a ship would carry off the criminals before a man could turn round.

At this the emperor wrathfully asked him whether his opinion had been invited; and the cunning Egyptian said to himself that Caracalla was anxious to spare the father and his sons for the daughter's sake. And yet Caesar would surely wish to keep them in safety, to have some hold over the girl; so he lied with a bold face, affirming that, in obedience to the law of the land, he had removed Heron and Philip, at any rate for the moment, beyond the reach of Caesar's mercy. They had in the course of the night been placed on board a galley and were now on the way to Sardinia. But a swift vessel should presently be sent to overtake it and bring them back.

And the informer was right, for Caesar's countenance brightened. He did, indeed, blame the Egyptian's overhasty action; but he gave no orders for following up the galley.

Then, after reflecting for a short time, he said:

"I do not find in either of you what I require; but at a pinch we are fain to eat moldy bread, so I must need choose between you two. The one who first brings me that clay figure, and the man who modeled it, in chains and bonds, shall be appointed chief of the night-watch."

Meanwhile Alexander had entered the room. As soon as Caracalla saw him, he beckoned to him, and the artist informed him that he had made good use of his time and had much to communicate. Then he humbly inquired as to the clay figure of which Caesar was speaking, and Caracalla referred him to Zminis. The Egyptian repeated what the Magian had told him.

Alexander listened calmly; but when Zminis ceased speaking, the artist took a deep breath, drew himself up, and pointing a contemptuous finger at the spy, as if his presence poisoned the air, he said: "It is that fellow's fault, great Caesar, if the citizens of my native town dare commit such crimes. He torments and persecutes them in your name. How many a felony has been committed here, merely to scoff at him and his creatures, and to keep them on the alert! We are a light-headed race. Like children, we love to do the forbidden thing, so long as it is no stain on our honor. But that wretch treats all laughter and the most innocent fun as a crime, or so interprets it that it seems so. From this malignant delight in the woes of others, and in the hope of rising higher in office, that wicked man has brought misery on hundreds. It has all been done in thy great name, O Caesar! No man has raised you up more foes than this wretch, who undermines your security instead of protecting it."

Here Zminis, whose swarthy face had become of ashy paleness, broke out in a hoarse tone: "I will teach you, and the whole rabble of traitors at your back—"

But Caesar wrathfully commanded him to be silent, and Alexander quietly went on: "You can threaten, and you will array all your slanderous arts against us, I know you. But here sits a sovereign who protects the innocent—and I and mine are innocent. He will set his heel on your head when he knows you—the curse of this city—for the adder that you are! He is deceiving you now in small things, great Caesar, and later he will deceive you in greater ones. Listen now how he has lied to you. He says he discovered a caricature of your illustrious person in the guise of a soldier. Why, then, did he not bring it away from the place where it could only excite disaffection, and might even mislead those who should see it into the belief that your noble person was that of a dwarf? The answer is self-evident. He left it to betray others into further mockery, to bring them to ruin."

Caesar had listened with approval, and now sternly asked the Egyptian:

"Did you see the image?"

"In the Elephant tavern!" yelled the man.

But Alexander shook his head doubtfully, and begged permission to ask the Egyptian a question. This was granted, and the artist inquired whether the soldier stood alone.

"So far as I remember, yes," replied Zminis, almost beside himself.

"Then your memory is as false as your soul!" Alexander shouted in his face, "for there was another figure by the soldier's side. The clay, still wet, clung to the same board as the figure of the soldier, modeled by the same hand. No, no, my crafty fellow, you will not catch the workman; for, being warned, he is already on the high-seas."

"It is false!" shrieked Zminis.

"That remains to be proved," said Alexander, scornfully.—"Allow me now, great Caesar, to show you the figures. They have been brought by my orders, and are in the anteroom-carefully covered up, of course, for the fewer the persons who see them the better."

Caracalla nodded his consent, and Alexander hurried away; the despot heaping abuse on Zminis, and demanding why he had not at once had the images removed. The Egyptian now confessed that he had only heard of the caricature from a friend, and declared that if he had seen it he should have destroyed it on the spot. Macrinus here tried to excuse the spy, by remarking that this zealous official had only tried to set his services in a favorable light.

The falsehood could not be approved, but was excusable. But he had scarcely finished speaking, when his opponent, the praetor, Lucius Priscillianus, observed, with a gravity he but rarely displayed:

"I should have thought that it was the first duty of the man who ought to be Caesar's mainstay and representative here, to let his sovereign hear nothing but the undistorted truth. Nothing, it seems to me, can be less excusable than a lie told to divine Caesar's face!"

A few courtiers, who were out of the prefect's favor, as well as the high-priest of Serapis, agreed with the speaker. Caracalla, however, paid no heed to them, but sat with his eyes fixed on the door, deeply wounded in his vanity by the mere existence of such a caricature.

He had not long to wait. But when the wrapper was taken off the clay figures, he uttered a low snarl, and his flushed face turned pale. Sounds of indignation broke from the bystanders; the blood rose to his cheeks again, and, shaking his fist, he muttered unintelligible threats, while his eyes wandered again and again to the caricatures. They attracted his attention more than all else, and as in an April day the sky is alternately dark and bright, so red and white alternated in his face. Then, while Alexander replied to a few questions, and assured him that the host of the "Elephant" had been very angry, and had gladly handed them over to him to be destroyed, Caracalla seemed to become accustomed to them, for he gazed at them more calmly, and tried to affect indifference. He inquired of Philostratus, as though he wished to be informed, whether he did not think that the artist who had modeled these figures must be a very clever follow; and when the philosopher assented conditionally, he declared that he saw some resemblance to himself—in the features of the apple-dealer. And then he pointed to his own straight legs, only slightly disfigured by an injury to the ankle, to show how shamefully unfair it was to compare them with the lower limbs of a misshapen dwarf. Finally, the figure of the apple-dealer—a hideous pygmy form, with the head of an old man, like enough to his own—roused his curiosity. What was the point of this image? What peculiarity was it intended to satirize? The basket which hung about the neck of the figure was full of fruit, and the object he held in his hand might be an apple, or might be anything else.

With eager and constrained cheerfulness, he inquired the opinion of his "friends," treating as sheer flattery a suggestion from his favorite, Theocritus, that this was not an apple-dealer, but a human figure, who, though but a dwarf in comparison with the gods, nevertheless endowed the world with the gifts of the immortals.

Alexander and Philostratus could offer no explanation; but when the proconsul, Julius Paulinus, observed that the figure was offering the apples for money, as Caesar offered the Roman citizenship to the provincials, he knew for what, Caracalla nodded agreement.

He then provisionally appointed Aristides to the coveted office. The Egyptian should be informed as to his fate. When the prefect was about to remove the figures, Caesar hastily forbade it, and ordered the bystanders to withdraw. Alexander alone was commanded to remain. As soon as they were together, Caesar sprang up and vehemently demanded to know what news he had brought. But the young man hesitated to begin his report. Caracalla, of his own accord, pledged his word once more to keep his oath, and then Alexander assured him that he knew no more than Caesar who were the authors of the epigrams which he had picked up here and there; and, though the satire they contained was venomous in some cases, still he, the sovereign of the world, stood so high that he could laugh them to scorn, as Socrates had laughed when Aristophanes placed him on the stage.

Caesar declared that he scorned these flies, but that their buzzing annoyed him.

Alexander rejoiced at this, and only expressed his regret that most of the epigrams he had collected turned on the death of Caesar's brother Geta. He knew now that it was rash to condemn a deed which—

Here Caesar interrupted him, for he could not long remain quiet, saying sternly:

"The deed was needful, not for me, but for the empire, which is dearer to me than father, mother, or a hundred brothers, and a thousand times dearer than men's opinions. Let me hear in what form the witty natives of this city express their disapproval."

This sounded so dignified and gracious that Alexander ventured to repeat a distich which he had heard at the public baths, whither he had first directed his steps. It did not, however, refer to the murder of Geta, but to the mantle-like garment to which Caesar owed the nickname of Caracalla. It ran thus:

"Why should my lord Caracalla affect a garment so ample?
'Tis that the deeds are many of evil he needs to conceal."

At this Caesar laughed, saying: "Who is there that has nothing to conceal? The lines are not amiss. Hand me your tablets; if the others are no worse—"

"But they are," Alexander exclaimed, anxiously, and I only regret that I should be the instrument of your tormenting yourself—"

"Tormenting?" echoed Caesar, disdainfully. "The verses amuse me, and I find them most edifying. That is all. Hand me the tablets."

The command was so positive, that Alexander drew out the little diptych, with the remark that painters wrote badly, and that what he had noted down was only intended to aid his memory. The idea that Caesar should hear a few home-truths through him had struck him as pleasant, but now the greatness of the risk was clear to him. He glanced at the scrawled characters, and it occurred to him that he had intended to change the word dwarf in one line to Caesar, and to keep the third and most trenchant epigram from the emperor. The fourth and last was very innocent, and he had meant to read it last, to mollify him. So he did not wish to show the tablets. But, as he was about to take them back, Caracalla snatched them from his hand and read with some difficulty:

> "Fraternal love was once esteemed
> A virtue even in the great,
>
> And Philadelphos then was deemed
> A name to grace a potentate.
> But now the dwarf upon the throne,
> By murder of his mother's son,
> As Misadelphos must be known."

"Indeed!" murmured Caesar, with a pale face, and then he went on in a low, sullen tone: "Always the same story—my brother, and my small stature. In this town they follow the example of the barbarians, it would seem, who choose the tallest and broadest of their race to be king. If the third epigram has nothing else in it, the shallow wit of your fellow-citizens is simply tedious.—Now, what have we next? Trochaics! Hardly anything new, I fear!—There is the water-jar. I will drink; fill the cup." But Alexander did not immediately obey the command so hastily given; assuring Caesar that he could not possibly read the writing, he was about to take up the tablets. But Caesar laid his hand on them, and said, imperiously: "Drink! Give me the cup."

He fixed his eyes on the wax, and with difficulty deciphered the clumsy scrawl in which Alexander had noted down the following lines, which he had heard at the "Elephant"

> "Since on earth our days are numbered,
> Ask me not what deeds of horror
> Stain the hands of fell Tarautas.
> Ask me of his noble actions,
> And with one short word I answer,
> 'None!'-replying to your question
> With no waste of precious hours."

Alexander meanwhile had done Caracalla's bidding, and when he had replaced the jar on its stand and returned to Caesar, he was horrified; for the emperor's head and arms were shaking and struggling to and fro, and at his feet lay the two halves of the wax tablets which he had torn apart when the convulsion came on. He foamed at the mouth, with low moans, and, before Alexander could prevent him, racked with pain and seeking for some support, he had set his teeth in the arm of the seat off which he was slipping. Greatly shocked, and full of sincere pity, Alexander tried to raise him; but the lion, who perhaps suspected the artist of having been the cause of this sudden attack, rose on his feet with a roar, and the young man would have had no chance of his life if the beast had not happily been chained down after his meal. With much presence of mind, Alexander sprang behind the chair and dragged it, with the unconscious man who served him as a shield, away from the angry brute.

Galen had urged Caesar to avoid excess in wine and violent emotions, and the wisdom of the warning was sufficiently proved by the attack which had seized him with such fearful violence, just when Caracalla had neglected it in both particulars. Alexander had to exert all the strength of his muscles, practised in the wrestling-school, to hold the sufferer on his seat, for his strength, which was not small, was doubled by the demons of epilepsy. In an instant the whole Court had rushed to the spot on hearing the lion's roar of rage, which grew louder and louder, and could be heard at no small distance, and then Alexander's shout for help. But the private physician and Epagathos, the chamberlain, would allow no one to enter the room; only old Adventus, who was half blind, was permitted to assist them in succoring the sufferer. He had been raised by Caracalla from the humble office of letter-carrier to the highest dignities and the office of his private chamberlain; but the leech availed himself by preference of the assistance of this experienced and quiet man, and between them they soon brought Caesar to his senses. Caesar then lay pale and exhausted on a couch which had hastily been arranged, his eyes fixed on vacancy, scarcely able to move a finger. Alexander held his trembling hand, and when the physician, a stout man of middle age, took the artist's place and bade him retire, Caracalla, in a low voice, desired him to remain.

As soon as Caesar's suspended faculties were fully awake again, he turned to the cause of his attack. With a look of pain and entreaty he desired Alexander to give him the tablets once more; but the artist assured him— and Caracalla seemed not sorry to believe—that he had crushed the wax in his convulsion. The sick man himself no doubt felt that such food was too strong for him. After he had remained staring at nothing in silence for some time, he began again to speak of the gibes of the Alexandrians. Surrounded as he was by servile favorites, whose superior he was in gifts and intellect, what had here come under his notice seemed to interest him above measure.

He desired to know where and from whom the painter had got these epigrams. But again Alexander declared that he did not know the names of the authors; that he had found one at the public baths, the second in a tavern, and the third at a hairdresser's shop. Caesar looked sadly at the youth's abundant brown curls which had been freshly oiled, and said: "Hair is like the other good gifts of life. It remains fine only with the healthy. You, happy rascal, hardly know what sickness means!" Then again he sat staring in silence, till he suddenly started up and asked Alexander, as Philostratus had yesterday asked Melissa:

"Do you and your sister belong to the Christians?"

When he vehemently denied it, Caracalla went on: "And yet these epigrams show plainly enough how the Alexandrians feel toward me. Melissa, too, is a daughter of this town, and when I remember that she could bring herself to pray for me, then—My nurse, who was the best of women, was a Christian. I learned from her the doctrine of loving our enemies and praying for those who despitefully treat us. I always regarded it as impossible; but now—your sister—What I was saying just now about the hair and good health reminds me of another speech of the Crucified one which my nurse often repeated— how long ago!—'To him that hath shall be given, and from him that hath not shall be taken even that which he hath.' How cruel and yet how wise, how terribly striking and true! A healthy man! What more can he want, and what abundant gifts that best of all gifts will gain for him! If he is visited by infirmity—only look at me!—how much misery I have suffered from this curse, terrible enough in itself, and tainting everything with the bitterness of wormwood!"

He laughed softly but scornfully, and continued: "But I! I am the sovereign of the universe. I have so much—oh yes, so much!—and for that reason more shall be given to me, and my wildest wishes shall be satisfied!"

"Yes, my liege!" interrupted Alexander, eagerly. "After pain comes pleasure!

'Live, love, drink, and rejoice,
And wreath thyself with me!'

sings Sappho, and it is not a bad plan to follow Anakreon's advice, even at the present day. Think of the short suffering which now and then embitters for you the sweet cup of life, as being the ring of Polykrates, with which you appease the envy of the gods who have given you so much. In your place, eternal gods! how I would enjoy the happy hours of health, and show the immortals and mortals alike how much true and real pleasure power and riches can procure!"

The emperor's weary eyes brightened, and with the cry—

"So will I! I am still young, and I have the power!" he started suddenly to his feet. But he sank back again directly on the couch, shaking his head as if to say, "There, you see what a state I am in!" The fate of this unhappy man touched Alexander's heart even more deeply than before.

His youthful mind, which easily received fresh impressions, forgot the deeds of blood and shame which stained the soul of this pitiable wretch. His artistic mind was accustomed to apprehend what he saw with his whole soul and without secondary considerations, as if it stood there to be painted; and the man that lay before him was to him at that moment only a victim whom a cruel fate had defrauded of the greatest pleasures in life. He also remembered how shamelessly he and others had mocked at Caesar. Perhaps Caracalla had really spilled most of the blood to serve the welfare and unity of the empire.

He, Alexander, was not his judge.

If Glaukias had seen the object of his derision lying thus, it certainly would never have occurred to him to represent him as a pygmy monster. No, no! Alexander's artistic eye knew the difference well between the beautiful and the ugly—and the exhausted man lying on the divan, was no hideous dwarf. A dreamy languor spread over his nobly chiselled features An expression of pain but rarely passed over them, and Caesar's whole appearance reminded the painter of the fine Ephesian gladiator hallistos as he lay on the sand, severely wounded after his last fight, awaiting the death-stroke. He would have liked to hasten home and fetch his materials to paint the likeness of the misjudged man, and to show it to the scoffers.

He stood silent, absorbed in studying the quiet face so finely formed by Nature and so pathetic to look at. No thoroughly depraved miscreant could look like that. Yet it was like a peaceful sea: when the hurricane should break loose, what a boiling whirl of gray, hissing, tossing, foaming waves would disfigure the peaceful, smooth, glittering surface!

And suddenly the emperor's features began to show signs of animation. His eye, but now so dull, shone more brightly, and he cried out, as if the long silence had scarcely broken the thread of his ideas, but in a still husky voice:

"I should like to get up and go with you, but I am still too weak. Do you go now, my friend, and bring me back fresh news."

Alexander then begged him to consider how dangerous every excitement would be for him; yet Caracalla exclaimed, eagerly:

"It will strengthen me and dome good! Everything that surrounds me is so hollow, so insipid, so contemptible—what I hear is so small. A strong, highly spiced word, even if it is sharp, refreshes me—When you have finished a picture, do you like to hear nothing but how well your friends can flatter?"

The artist thought he understood Caesar. True to his nature, always hoping for the best, he thought that, as the severe judgment of the envious had often done him (Alexander) good, so the sharp satire of the Alexandrians would lead Caracalla to introspection and greater moderation; he only resolved to tell the sufferer nothing further that was merely insulting.

When he bade him farewell, Caracalla glanced up at him with such a look of pain that the artist longed to give him his hand, and speak to him with real affection. The tormenting headache which followed each convulsion had again come on, and Caesar submitted without resistance to what the physician prescribed.

Alexander asked old Adventus at the door if he did not think that the terrible attack had been brought on by annoyance at the Alexandrians' satire, and if it would not be advisable in the future not to allow such things to reach the emperor's ear; but the man, looking at him in surprise with his half-blind eyes, replied with a brutal want of sympathy that disgusted the youth: "Drinking brought on the attack. What makes him ill are stronger things than words. If you yourself, young man, do not suffer for Alexandrian wit, it will certainly not hurt Caesar!"

Alexander turned his back indignantly on the chamberlain, and he became so absorbed in wondering how it was possible that the emperor, who was cultivated and appreciated what was beautiful, could have dragged out of the dust and kept near him two such miserable 'creatures as Theocritus and this old man, that Philostratus, who met him in the next room, had almost to shout at him.

Philostratus informed him that Melissa was staying with the chief priest's wife; but just as he was about to inquire curiously what had passed between the audacious painter and Caesar—for even Philostratus was a courtier—he was called away to Caracalla.

CHAPTER XIX.

In one of the few rooms of his vast palace which the chief priest had reserved for the accommodation of the members of his own household, the youth was received by Melissa, Timotheus's wife Euryale, and the lady Berenike.

This lady was pleased to see the artist again to whom she was indebted for the portrait of her daughter. She had it now in her possession once more, for Philostratus had had it taken back to her house while the emperor was at his meal.

She rested on a sofa, quite worn out. She had passed through hours of torment; for her concern about Melissa, who had become very dear to her, had given her much more anxiety than even the loss of her beloved picture. Besides, the young girl was to her for the moment the representative of her sex, and the danger of seeing this pure, sweet creature exposed to the will of a licentious tyrant drove her out of her senses, and her lively fancy had resulted in violent outbreaks of indignation. She now proposed all sorts of schemes, of which Euryale, the more prudent but not less warm-hearted wife of the chief priest, demonstrated the impossibility.

Like Berenike, a tender-hearted woman, whose smooth, brown hair had already begun to turn gray, she had also lost her only child. But years had passed since then, and she had accustomed herself to seek comfort in the care of the sick and wretched. She was regarded all over the city as the providence of all in need, whatever their condition and faith. Where charity was to be bestowed on a large scale—if hospitals or almshouses were to be erected or endowed—she was appealed to first, and if she promised her quiet but valuable assistance, the result was at once secured. For, besides her own and her husband's great riches, this lady of high position, who was honored by all, had the purses of all the heathens and Christians in the city at her disposal; both alike considered that she belonged to them; and the latter, although she only held with them in secret, had the better right.

At home, the society of distinguished men afforded her the greatest pleasure. Her husband allowed her complete freedom; although he, as the chief Greek priest of the city, would have preferred that she should not also have had among her most constant visitors so many learned Christians. But the god whom he served united in his own person most of the others; and the mysteries which he superintended taught that even Serapis was only a symbolical embodiment of the universal soul, fulfilling its eternal existence by perpetually re-creating itself under constant and immutable laws. A portion of that soul, which dwelt in all created things, had its abode in each human being, to return to the divine source after death. Timotheus firmly clung to this pantheist creed; still, he held the honorable post of head of the

Museum—in the place of the Roman priest of Alexander, a man of less learning—and was familiar not only with the tenets of his heathen predecessors, but with the sacred scriptures of the Jews and Christians; and in the ethics of these last he found much which met his views.

He, who, at the Museum, was counted among the skeptics, liked biblical sentences, such as "All is vanity," and "We know but in part." The command to love your neighbor, to seek peace, to thirst after truth, the injunction to judge the tree by its fruit, and to fear more for the soul than the body, were quite to his mind.

He was so rich that the gifts of the visitors to the temple, which his predecessors had insisted on, were of no importance to him. Thus he mingled a great deal that was Christian with the faith of which he was chief minister and guardian. Only the conviction with which men like Clemens and Origen, who were friends of his wife, declared that the doctrine to which they adhered was the only right one—was, in fact, the truth itself—seemed to the skeptic "foolishness."

His wife's friends had converted his brother Zeno to Christianity; but he had no need to fear lest Euryale should follow them. She loved him too much, and was too quiet and sensible, to be baptized, and thus expose him, the heathen high-priest, to the danger of being deprived of the power which she knew to be necessary to his happiness.

Every Alexandrian was free to belong to any other than the heathen creeds, and no one had taken offence at his skeptical writings. When Euryale acted like the best of the Christian women, he could not take it amiss; and he would have scorned to blame her preference for the teaching of the crucified God.

As to Caesar's character he had not yet made up his mind.

He had expected to find him a half-crazy villain, and his rage after he had heard the epigram against himself, left with the rope, had strengthened the chief priest's opinion. But since then he had heard of much that was good in him; and Timotheus felt sure that his judgment was unbiased by the high esteem Caesar showed to him, while he treated others like slaves. His improved opinion had been raised by the intercourse he had held with Caesar. The much-abused man had on these occasions shown that he was not only well educated but also thoughtful; and yesterday evening, before Caracalla had gone to rest exhausted, the high-priest, with his wise experience, had received exactly the same impressions as the easily influenced artist; for Caesar had bewailed his sad fate in pathetic terms, and confessed himself indeed deeply guilty, but declared that he had intended to act for the best, had sacrificed fortune, peace of mind, and comfort to the welfare of the state. His keen eye had marked the evils of the time, and he had acknowledged that his efforts to extirpate the old maladies in order to make room for better things had been a failure, and that, instead of earning thanks, he had drawn down on himself the hatred of millions.

It was for this reason that Timotheus, on rejoining his household, had assured them that, as he thought over this interview, he expected something good—yes, perhaps the best—from the young criminal in the purple.

But the lady Berenike had declared with scornful decision that Caracalla had deceived her brother-in-law; and when Alexander likewise tried to say a word for the sufferer, she got into a rage and accused him of foolish credulity.

Melissa, who had already spoken in favor of the emperor, agreed, in spite of the matron, with her brother. Yes, Caracalla had sinned greatly, and his conviction that Alexander's soul lived in him and Roxana's in her was foolish enough; but the marvelous likeness to her of the portrait on the gem would astonish any one. That good and noble impulses stirred his soul she was certain. But Berenike only shrugged her shoulders contemptuously; and when the chief priest remarked that yesterday evening Caracalla had in fact not been in a position to attend a feast, and that a portion, at least, of his other offenses might certainly be put down to the charge of his severe suffering, the lady exclaimed:

"And is it also his bodily condition that causes him to fill a house of mourning with festive uproar? I am indifferent as to what makes him a malefactor. For my part, I would sooner abandon this dear child to the care of a criminal than to that of a madman."

But the chief priest and the brother and sister both declared Caesar's mind to be as sound and sharp as any one's; and Timotheus asked who, at the present time, was without superstition, and the desire of communicating with departed souls. Still the matron would not allow herself to be persuaded, and after the chief priest had been called away to the service of the god, Euryale reproved her sister-in-law for her too great zeal. When the wisdom of hoary old age and impetuous youth agree in one opinion, it is commonly the right one.

"And I maintain," cried Berenike—and her large eyes flamed angrily—" it is criminal to ignore my advice. Fate has robbed you as well as me of a dear child. I will not also lose this one, who is as precious to me as a daughter."

Melissa bent over the lady's hands and kissed them gratefully, exclaiming with tearful eyes, "But he has been very good to me, and has assured me-"

"Assured!" repeated Berenike disdainfully. She then drew the young girl impetuously toward her, kissed her on her forehead, placed her hands on her head as if to protect her, and turned to the artist as she continued:

"I stand by what I recommended before. This very night Melissa must get far away from here. You, Alexander, must accompany her. My own ship, the 'Berenike and Korinna'—Seleukus gave it to me and my daughter—is ready to start. My sister lives in Carthage. Her husband, the first man in the city, is my friend. You will find protection and shelter in their house."

"And how about our father and Philip?" interrupted Alexander. "If we follow your advice, it is certain death to them!"

The matron laughed scornfully.

"And that is what you expect from this good, this great and noble sovereign!"

"He proves himself full of favors to his friends," answered Alexander, "but woe betide those who offend him!"

Berenike looked thoughtfully at the ground, and added, more quietly:

"Then try first to release your people, and afterward embark on my ship. It shall be ready for you. Melissa will use it, I know.—My veil, child! The chariot waits for me at the Temple of Isis.—You will accompany me there, Alexander, and we will drive to the harbor. There I will introduce you to the captain. It will be wise. Your father and brother are dearer to you than your sister; she is more important to me. If only I could go away myself—away from here, from the desolate house, and take her with me!"

And she raised her arm, as if she would throw a stone into the distance.

She impetuously embraced the young girl, took leave of her sister-in-law, and left the room with Alexander.

Directly Euryale was alone with Melissa, she comforted the girl in her kind, composed manner; for the unhappy matron's gloomy presentiments had filled Melissa with fresh anxieties.

And what had she not gone through during the day!

Soon after her perilous interview with Caracalla, Timotheus, with the chief of the astrologers from the Serapeum, and the emperor's astronomer, had come to her, to ask her on what day and at what hour she was born. They also inquired concerning the birthdays of her parents, and other events of her life. Timotheus had informed her that the emperor had ordered them to cast her nativity.

Soon after dinner she had gone, accompanied by the lady Berenike, who had found her at the chief priest's house, to visit her lover in the sick- rooms of the Serapeum. Thankful and happy, she had found him with fully recovered consciousness, but the physician and the freedman Andreas, whom she met at the door of the chamber, had impressed on her the importance of avoiding all excitement. So it had not been possible for her to tell him what had happened to her people, or of the perilous step she had taken in order to save them. But Diodoros had talked of their wedding, and Andreas could confirm the fact that Polybius wished to see it celebrated as soon as possible.

Several pleasant subjects were discussed; but between whiles Melissa had to dissemble and give evasive answers to Diodoros's questions as to whether she had already arranged with her brother and friends who should be the youths and maidens to form the wedding procession, and sing the hymeneal song.

As the two whispered to one another and looked tenderly at each other— for Diodoros had insisted on her allowing him to kiss not only her hands but also her sweet red lips—Berenike had pictured her dead daughter in Melissa's place. What a couple they would have been! How proudly and gladly she would have led them to the lovely villa at Kanopus, which her husband and she had rebuilt and decorated with the idea that some day Korinna, her husband, and—if the gods should grant it—their children, might inhabit it! But even Melissa and Diodoros made a fine couple, and she tried with all her heart not to grudge her all the happiness that she had wished for her own child.

When it was time to depart, she joined the hands of the betrothed pair, and called down a blessing from the gods.

Diodoros accepted this gratefully.

He only knew that this majestic lady had made Melissa's acquaintance through Alexander, and had won her affection, and he encouraged the impression that this woman, whose Juno-like beauty haunted him, had visited him on his bed of sickness in the place of his long-lost mother.

Outside the sick-room Andreas again met Melissa, and, after she had told him of her visit to the emperor, he impressed on her eagerly on no account to obey the tyrant's call again. Then he had promised to hide her securely, either on Zeno's estate or else in the house of another friend, which was difficult of access. When Dame Berenike had again, and with particular eagerness, suggested her ship, Andreas had exclaimed:

"In the garden, on the ship, under the earth—only not back to Caesar!"

The last question of the freedman's, as to whether she had meditated further on his discourse, had reminded her of the sentence, "The fullness of the time is come"; and afterward the thought occurred to her, again and again, that in the course of the next few hours some decisive event would happen to her, "fulfilling the time," as Andreas expressed it.

When, therefore, somewhat later, she was alone with the chief priest's wife, who had concluded her comforting, pious exhortations, Melissa asked the lady Euryale whether she had ever heard the sentence, "When the fullness of the time is come."

At this the lady cried, gazing at the girl with surprised inquiry:

"Are you, then, after all, connected with the Christians?"

"Certainly not," answered the young girl, firmly. "I heard it accidentally, and Andreas, Polybius's freedman, explained it to me."

"A good interpreter," replied the elder lady. "I am only an ignorant woman; yet, child, even I have experienced that a day, an hour, comes to every man in the course of his life in which he afterward sees that the time was fulfilled. As the drops become mingled with the stream, so at that moment the things we have done and thought unite to carry us on a new current, either to salvation or perdition. Any moment may bring the crisis; for that reason the Christians are right when they call on one another to watch. You also must keep your eyes open. When the time—who knows how soon?—is fulfilled for you, it will determine the good or evil of your whole life."

"An inward voice tells me that also," answered Melissa, pressing her hands on her panting bosom. "Just feel how my heart beats!"

Euryale, smiling, complied with this wish, and as she did so she shuddered. How pure and lovable was this young creature; and Melissa looked to her like a lamb that stood ready to hasten trustfully to meet the wolf!

At last she led her guest into the room where supper was prepared.

The master of the house would not be able to share it, and while the two women sat opposite one another, saying little, and scarcely touching either food or drink, Philostratus was announced.

He came as messenger from Caracalla, who wished to speak to Melissa.

"At this hour? Never, never! It is impossible!" exclaimed Euryale, who was usually so calm; but Philostratus declared, nevertheless, that denial was useless. The emperor was suffering particularly severely, and begged to remind Melissa of her promise to serve him gladly if he required her. Her presence, he assured Euryale, would do the sick man good, and he guaranteed that, so long as Caesar was tormented by this unbearable pain, the young woman had nothing to fear.

Melissa, who had risen from her seat when the philosopher had entered, exclaimed:

"I am not afraid, and will go with you gladly—"

"Quite right, child," answered Philostratus, affectionately. Euryale, however, found it difficult to keep back her tears while she stroked the girl's hair and arranged the folds of her garment. When at last she said good-by to Melissa and was embracing her, she was reminded of the farewell she had taken, many years ago, of a Christian friend before she was led away by the lictors to martyrdom in the circus. Finally, she whispered something in the philosopher's ear, and received from him the promise to return with Melissa as soon as possible.

Philostratus was, in fact, quite easy. Just before, Caracalla's helpless glance had met his sympathizing gaze, and the suffering Caesar had said nothing to him but:

"O Philostratus, I am in such pain!" and these words still rang in the ears of this warm-hearted man.

While he was endeavoring to comfort the emperor, Caesar's eyes had fallen on the gem, and he asked to see it. He gazed at it attentively for some time, and when he returned it to the philosopher he had ordered him to fetch the prototype of Roxana.

Closely enveloped in the veil which Euryale had placed on her head, Melissa passed from room to room, keeping near to the philosopher.

Wherever she appeared she heard murmuring and whispering that troubled her, and tittering followed her from several of the rooms as she left them; even from the large hall where the emperor's friends awaited his orders in numbers, she heard a loud laugh that frightened and annoyed her.

She no longer felt as unconstrained as she had been that morning when she had come before Caesar. She knew that she would have to be on her guard; that anything, even the worst, might be expected from him. But as Philostratus described to her, on the way, how terribly the unfortunate man suffered, her tender heart was again drawn to him, to whom—as she now felt—she was bound by an indefinable tie. She, if any one, as she repeated to herself, was able to help him; and her desire to put the truth of this conviction to the proof—for she could only regard it as too amazing to be grounded in fact—was seconded by the less disinterested hope that, while attending on the sufferer, she might find an opportunity of effecting the release of her father and brother.

Philostratus went on to announce her arrival, and she, while waiting, tried to pray to the manes of her mother; but, before she could sufficiently collect her thoughts, the door opened. Philostratus silently beckoned to her, and she stepped into the tablinum, which was but dimly lighted by a few lamps.

Caracalla was still resting here; for every movement increased the pain that tormented him.

How quiet it was! She thought she could hear her own heart beating.

Philostratus remained standing by the door, but she went on tiptoe toward the couch, fearing her light footsteps might disturb the emperor. Yet before she had reached the divan she stopped still, and then she heard the plaintive rattle in the sufferer's throat, and from the background of the room the easy breathing of the burly physician and of old Adventus, both of whom had fallen asleep; and then a peculiar tapping. The lion beat the floor with his tail with pleasure at recognizing her.

This noise attracted the invalid's attention, and when he opened his closed eyes and saw Melissa, who was anxiously watching all his movements, he called to her lightly with his hand on his brow:

"The animal has a good memory, and greets you in my name. You were sure to come—, I knew it!"

The young girl stepped nearer to him, and answered, kindly, "Since you needed me, I gladly followed Philostratus."

"Because I needed you?" asked the emperor.

"Yes," she replied, "because you require nursing."

"Then, to keep you, I shall wish to be ill often," he answered, quickly; but he added, sadly, "only not so dreadfully ill as I have been to-day."

One could hear how laborious talking was to him, and the few words he had sought and found, in order to say something kind to Melissa, had so hurt his shattered nerves and head that he sank back, gasping, on the cushions.

Then for some time all was quiet, until Caracalla took his hand from his forehead and continued, as if in excuse:

"No one seems to know what it is. And if I talk ever so softly, every word vibrates through my brain."

"Then you must not speak," interrupted Melissa, eagerly. "If you want anything, only make signs. I shall understand you without words, and the quieter it is here the better."

"No, no; you must speak," begged the invalid. "When the others talk, they make the beating in my head ten times worse, and excite me; but I like to hear your voice."

"The beating?" interrupted Melissa, in whom this word awoke old memories. "Perhaps you feel as if a hammer was hitting you over the left eye?

"If you move rapidly, does it not pierce your skull, and do you not feel as sick as if you were on the rocking sea?"

"Then you also know this torment?" asked Caracalla, surprised; but she answered, quietly, that her mother had suffered several times from similar headaches, and had described them to her.

Caesar sank back again on the pillows, moved his dry lips, and glanced toward the drink which Galen had prescribed for him; and Melissa, who almost as a child had long nursed a dear invalid, guessed what he wanted, brought him the goblet, and gave him a draught.

Caracalla rewarded her with a grateful look. But the physic only seemed to increase the pain. He lay there panting and motionless, until, trying to find a new position, he groaned, lightly:

"It is as if iron was being hammered here. One would think others might hear it."

At the same time he seized the girl's hand and placed it on his burning brow.

Melissa felt the pulse in the sufferer's temple throbbing hard and short against her fingers, as she had her mother's when she laid her cool hand on her aching forehead; and then, moved by the wish to comfort and heal, she let her right hand rest over the sick man's eyes. As soon as she felt one hand was hot, she put the other in its place; and it must have relieved the patient, for his moans ceased by degrees, and he finally said, gratefully:

"What good that does me! You are—I knew you would help me. It is already quite quiet in my brain. Once more your hand, dear girl!"

Melissa willingly obeyed him, and as he breathed more and more easily, she remembered that her mother's headache had often been relieved when she had placed her hand on her forehead. Caesar, now opening his eyes wide, and looking her full in the face, asked why she had not allowed him sooner to reap the benefit of this remedy.

Melissa slowly withdrew her hand, and with drooping eyes answered gently:

"You are the emperor, a man. . . and I. . . . But Caracalla interrupted her eagerly, and with a clear voice:

"Not so, Melissa! Do not you feel, like me, that something else draws us to one another, like what binds a man to his wife?-There lies the gem. Look at it once again—No, child, no! This resemblance is not mere accident. The short-sighted, might call it superstition or a vain illusion; I know better. At least a portion of Alexander's soul lives in this breast. A hundred signs—I will tell you about it later—make it a certainty to me. And yesterday morning. . . . I see it all again before me. . . . You stood above me, on the left, at a window. . . I looked up; . . our eyes met, and I felt in the depths of my heart a strange emotion. . . . I asked myself, silently, where I had seen that lovely face before. And the answer rang, you have already often met her; you know her!"

"My face reminded you of the gem," interrupted Melissa, disquieted.

"No, no," continued Caesar. "It was some thing else. Why had none of my many gems ever reminded me before of living people? Why did your picture, I know not how often, recur to my mind? And you? Only recollect what you have done for me. How marvelously we were brought together! And all this in the course of a single, short day. And you also. . . . I ask you, by all that is holy to you. . . Did you, after you saw me in the court of sacrifice, not think of me so often and so vividly that it astonished you?"

"You are Caesar," answered Melissa, with increasing anxiety.

"So you thought of my purple robes?" asked Caracalla, and his face clouded over; "or perhaps only of my power that might be fatal to your family? I will know. Speak the truth, girl, by the head of your father!"

Then Melissa poured forth this confession from her oppressed heart:

"Yes, I could not help remembering you constantly, . . . and I never saw you in purple, but just as you had stood there on the steps; . . . and then—ah! I have told you already how sorry I was for your sufferings. I felt as if . . . but how can I describe it truly?— as if you stood much nearer to me than the ruler of the world could to a poor, humble girl. It was . . . eternal gods! . . ."

She stopped short; for she suddenly recollected anxiously that this confession might prove fatal to her. The sentence about the time which should be fulfilled for each was ringing in her ears, and it seemed to her that she heard for the second time the lady Berenike's warning.

But Caracalla allowed her no time to think; for he interrupted her, greatly pleased, with the cry:

"It is true, then! The immortals have wrought as great a miracle in you as in me. We both owe them thanks, and I will show them how grateful I can be by rich sacrifices. Our souls, which destiny had already once united, have met again. That portion of the universal soul which of yore dwelt in Roxana, and now in you, Melissa, has also vanquished the pain which has embittered my life. . . You have proved it!—And now . . . it is beginning to throb again more violently—now—beloved and restored one, help me once more!"

Melissa perceived anxiously how the emperor's face had flushed again during this last vehement speech, and at the same time the pain had again contracted his forehead and eyes. And she obeyed his command, but this time only in shy submission. When she found that he became quieter, and the movement of her hand once more did him good, she recovered her presence of mind. She remembered how often the quiet application of her hand had helped her mother to sleep.

She therefore explained to Caracalla, in a low whisper directly he began to speak again, that her desire to give him relief would be vain if he did not keep his eyes and lips closed. And Caracalla yielded, while her hand moved as lightly over the brow of the terrible man as when years ago it had soothed her mother to sleep.

When the sufferer, after a little time, murmured, with closed eyes

"Perhaps I could sleep," she felt as if great happiness had befallen her.

She listened attentively to every breath, and looked as if spell-bound into his face, until she was quite sure that sleep had completely overcome Caesar.

She then crept gently on tiptoe to Philostratus, who had looked on in silent surprise at all that had passed between his sovereign and the girl. He, who was always inclined to believe in any miraculous cure, of which so many had been wrought by his hero Apollonius, thought he had actually witnessed one, and gazed with an admiration bordering on awe at the young creature who appeared to him to be a gracious instrument of the gods.

"Let me go now," Melissa whispered to her friend. "He sleeps, and will not wake for some time."

"At your command," answered the philosopher, respectfully. At the same moment a loud voice was heard from the next room, which Melissa recognized as her brother Alexander's, who impetuously insisted on his right of—being allowed at any time to see the emperor.

"He will wake him," murmured the philosopher, anxiously; but Melissa with prompt determination threw her veil over her head and went into the adjoining room.

Philostratus at first heard violent language issuing from the mouth of Theocritus and the other courtiers, and the artist's answers were not less passionate. Then he recognized Melissa's voice; and when quiet suddenly reigned on that side of the door, the young girl again crossed the threshold.

She glanced toward Caracalla to see if he still slept, and then, with a sigh of relief, beckoned to her friend, and begged him in a whisper to escort her past the staring men. Alexander followed them.

Anger and surprise were depicted on his countenance, which was usually so happy. He had come with a report which might very likely induce Caesar to order the release of his father and brother, and his heart had stood still with fear and astonishment when the favorite Theocritus had told him in the anteroom, in a way that made the blood rush into his face, that his sister had been for some time endeavoring to comfort the suffering emperor—and it was nearly midnight.

Quite beside himself, he wished to force his way into Caesar's presence, but Melissa had at that moment come out and stood in his way, and had desired him and the noble Romans, in such a decided and commanding tone, to lower their voices, that they and her brother were speechless.

What had happened to his modest sister during the last few days? Melissa giving him orders which he feebly obeyed! It seemed impossible! But there was something reassuring in her manner. She must certainly have thought it right to act thus, and it must have been worthy of her, or she would not have carried her charming head so high, or looked him so freely and calmly in the face.

But how had she dared to come between him and his duty to his father and brother?

While he followed her closely and silently through the imperial rooms, the implicit obedience he had shown her became more and more difficult to comprehend; and when at last they stood in the empty corridor which divided Caesar's quarters from those of the high-priest, and Philostratus had returned to his post at the side of his sovereign, he could hold out no longer, and cried to her indignantly:

"So far, I have followed you like a boy; I do not myself know why. But it is not yet too late to turn round; and I ask you, what gave you the right to prevent my doing my best for our people?"

"Your loud talking, that threatened to wake Caesar," she replied, seriously. "His sleeping could alone save me from watching by him the whole night."

Alexander then felt sorry he had been so foolishly turbulent, and after Melissa had told him in a few words what she had gone through in the last few hours he informed her of what had brought him to visit the emperor so late.

Johannes the lawyer, Berenike's Christian freedman, he began, had visited their father in prison and had heard the order given to place Heron and Philip as state prisoners and oarsmen on board a galley.

This had taken place in the afternoon, and the Christian had further learned that the prisoners would be led to the harbor two hours before sunset. This was the truth, and yet the infamous Zminis had assured the emperor, at noon, that their father and Philip were already far on their way to Sardinia. The worthless Egyptian had, then, lied to the emperor; and it would most likely cost the scoundrel his neck. But for this, there would have been time enough next day. What had brought him there at so late an hour was the desire to prevent the departure of the galley; for John had heard, from the Christian harbor-watch that the anchor was not yet weighed. The ship could therefore only get out to sea at sunrise; the chain that closed the harbor would not be opened till then. If the order to stop the galley came much after daybreak, she would certainly be by that time well under way, and their father and Philip might have succumbed to the hard rowing before a swift trireme could overtake and release them.

Melissa had listened to this information with mixed feelings. She had perhaps precipitated her father and brother into misery in order to save herself; for a terrible fate awaited the state-prisoners at the oars. And what could she do, an ignorant child, who was of so little use?

Andreas had told her that it was the duty of a Christian and of every good man, if his neighbor's welfare were concerned, to sacrifice his own fortunes; and for the happiness and lives of those dearest to her—for they, of all others, were her "neighbors"—she felt that she could do so. Perhaps she might yet succeed in repairing the mischief she had done when she had allowed the emperor to sleep without giving one thought to her father. Instead of waking him, she had misused her new power over her brother, and, by preventing his speaking, had perhaps frustrated the rescue of her people.

But idle lamenting was of as little use here as at any other time; so she resolutely drew her veil closer round her head and called to her brother, "Wait here till I return!"

"What are you going to do?" asked Alexander, startled.

"I am going back to the invalid," she explained, decisively.

On this her brother seized her arm, and, wildly excited, forbade this step in the name of his father.

But at his vehement shout, "I will not allow it!" she struggled to free herself, and cried out to him:

"And you? Did not you, whose life is a thousand times more important than mine, of your own free-will go into captivity and to death in order to save our father?"

"It was for my sake that he had been robbed of his freedom," interrupted Alexander; but she added, quickly:

"And if I had not thought only of myself, the command to release him and Philip would by this time have been at the harbor. I am going."

Alexander then took his hand from her arm, and exclaimed, as if urged by some internal force, "Well, then, go!"

"And you," continued Melissa, hastily, "go and seek the lady Euryale. She is expecting me. Tell her all, and beg her in my name to go to rest. Also tell her I remembered the sentence about the time, which was fulfilled. . . . Mark the words. If I am running again into danger, tell her that I do it because a voice says to me that it is right. And it is right, believe me, Alexander!"

The artist drew his sister to him and kissed her; yet she hardly understood his anxious good wishes; for his voice was choked by emotion.

He had taken it for granted that he should accompany her as far as the emperor's room, but she would not allow it. His reappearance would only lead to fresh quarrels.

He also gave in to this; but he insisted on returning here to wait for her.

After Melissa had vanished into Caesar's quarters he immediately carried out his sister's wish, and told the lady Euryale of all that had happened.

Encouraged by the matron, who was not less shocked than he had been at Melissa's daring, he returned to the anteroom, where, at first, greatly excited, he walked up and down, and then sank on a marble seat to wait for his sister. He was frequently overpowered by sleep. The things that cast a shadow on his sunny mind vanished from him, and a pleasing dream showed him, instead of the alarming picture which haunted him before sleeping, the beautiful Christian Agatha.

CHAPTER XX.

The waiting-room was empty when Melissa crossed it for the second time. Most of the emperor's friends had retired to rest or into the city when they had heard that Caesar slept; and the few who had remained behaved quietly when she appeared, for Philostratus had told them that the emperor held her in high esteem, as the only person who was able to give him comfort in his suffering by her peculiar and wonderful healing power.

In the tablinum, which had been converted into a sick-room, nothing was heard but the breathing and gentle snoring of the sleeping man. Even Philostratus was asleep on an arm-chair at the back of the room.

When the philosopher had returned, Caracalla had noticed him, and dozing, or perhaps in his dreams, he had ordered him to remain by him. So the learned man felt bound to spend the night there.

Epagathos, the freedman, was lying on a mattress from the dining-room; the corpulent physician slept soundly, and if he snored too loudly, old Adventus poked him and quietly spoke a word of warning to him. This man, who had formerly been a post messenger, was the only person who was conscious of Melissa's entrance; but he only blinked at her through his dim eyes, and, after he had silently considered why the young girl should have returned, he turned over in order to sleep himself; for he had come to the conclusion that this young, active creature would be awake and at hand if his master required anything.

His wondering as to why Melissa had returned, had led to many guesses, and had proved fruitless. "You can know nothing of women," was the end of his reflections, "if you do not know that what seems most improbable is what is most likely to be true. This maid is certainly not one of the flute-players or the like. Who knows what incomprehensible whim or freak may have brought her here? At any rate, it will be easier for her to keep her eyes open than it is for me."

He then signed to her and asked her quietly to fetch his cloak out of the next room, for his old body needed warmth; and Melissa gladly complied, and laid the caracalla over the old mans cold feet with obliging care.

She then returned to the side of the sick-bed, to wait for the emperor's awaking. He slept soundly; his regular breathing indicated this. The others also slept, and Adventus's light snore, mingling with the louder snoring of the physician, showed that he too had ceased to watch. The slumbering Philostratus now and then murmured incomprehensible words to himself; and the lion, who perhaps was dreaming of his freedom in his sandy home, whined low in his sleep.

She watched alone.

It seemed to her as if she were in the habitation of sleep, and as if phantoms and dreams were floating around her on the unfamiliar noises.

She was afraid, and the thought of being the only woman among so many men caused her extreme uneasiness.

She could not sit still.

Inaudibly as a shadow she approached the head of the sleeping emperor, holding her breath to listen to him. How soundly he slept! And she had come that she might talk to him. If his sleep lasted till sunrise, the pardon for her people would be too late, and her father and Philip, chained to a hard bench, would have to ply heavy oars as galley slaves by the side of robbers and murderers. How terribly then would her father's wish to use his strength be granted! Was Philip, the narrow-chested philosopher, capable of bearing the strain which had so often proved fatal to stronger men?

She must wake the dreaded man, the only man who could possibly help her.

She now raised her hand to lay it on his shoulder, but she half withdrew it.

It seemed to her as if it was not much less wicked to rob a sleeping man of his rest, his best cure, than to take the life of a living being. It was not too late yet, for the harbor-chain would not be opened till the October sun had risen. He might enjoy his slumbers a little longer.

With this conclusion she once more sank down and listened to the noises which broke the stillness of the night.

How hideous they were, how revolting they sounded! The vulgarest of the sleepers, old Adventus, absolutely sawed the air with his snoring.

The emperor's breathing was scarcely perceptible, and how nobly cut was the profile which she could see, the other side of his face leaning on the pillow! Had she any real reason to fear his awakening? Perhaps he was quite unlike what Berenike thought him to be. She remembered the sympathy she had felt for him when they had first met, and, in spite of all the trouble she had experienced since, she no longer felt afraid. A thought then occurred to her which was sufficient excuse for disturbing the sick man's sleep. If she delayed it, she would be making him guilty of a fresh crime by allowing two blameless men to perish in misery. But she would first convince herself whether the time was pressing. She looked out through the open window at the stars and across the open place lying at her feet. The third hour after midnight was past, and the sun would rise before long.

Down below all was quiet. Macrinus, the praetorian prefect, on hearing that the emperor had fallen into a refreshing sleep, in order that he might not be disturbed, had forbidden all loud signals, and ordered the camp to be closed to all the inhabitants of the city; so the girl heard nothing but the regular footsteps of the sentries and the shrieks of the owls returning to their nests in the roof of the Serapeum. The wind from the sea drove the clouds before it across the sky, and the plain covered with tents resembled a sea tossed into high white waves. The camp had been reduced during the afternoon; for Caracalla had carried out his threat of that morning by quartering a portion of the picked troops in the houses of the richest Alexandrians.

Melissa, bending far out, looked toward the north. The sea-breeze blew her hair into her face. Perhaps on the ocean whence it came the high waves would, in a few hours, be tossing the ship on which her father and brother, seated at the oar, would be toiling as disgraced galley-slaves. That must not, could not be!

Hark! what was that?

She heard a light whisper. In spite of strict orders, a loving couple were passing below. The wife of the centurion Martialis, who had been separated for some time from her husband, had at his entreaty come secretly from Ranopus, where she had charge of Seleukus's villa, to see him, as his services prevented his going so far away. They now stood whispering and making love in the shadow of the temple. Melissa could not hear what they said, yet it reminded her of the sacred night hour when she confessed her love to Diodoros. She felt as if she were standing by his bedside, and his faithful eyes met hers. She would not, for all that was best in the world, have awakened him yesterday at the Christian's house, though the awakening would have brought her fresh promises of love; and yet she was on the point of robbing another of his only cure, the sleep the gods had sent him. But then she loved Diodoros, and what was Caesar to her? It had been a matter of life and death with her lover, while disturbing Caracalla would only postpone his recovery a few hours at the utmost. It was she who had procured the imperial sleeper his rest, which she could certainly restore to him even if she now woke him. Just now she had vowed for the future not to care about her own welfare, and that had at first made her doubtful about Caracalla; but had it not really been exceedingly selfish to lose the time which could bring freedom to her father and brother, only to protect her own soul from the reproach of an easily forgiven wrong? With the question:

"What is your duty?" all doubts left her, and no longer on tiptoe, but with a firm, determined tread, she walked toward the slumberer's couch, and the outrage which she shrank from committing would, she saw, be a deed of kindness; for she found the emperor with perspiring brow groaning and frightened by a severe nightmare. He cried with the dull, toneless voice of one talking in his sleep, as if he saw her close by:

"Away, mother, I say! He or I! Out of the way! You will not? But I, I—If you—"

At the same he threw up his hands and gave a dull, painful cry.

"He is dreaming of his brother's murder," rushed through Melissa's mind, and in the same instant she laid her hand on his arm and with urgent entreaty cried in his ear: "Wake up, Caesar, I implore you! Great Caesar, awake!"

Then he opened his eyes, and a low, prolonged "Ah!" rang from his tortured breast.

He then, with a deep breath and perplexed glance, looked round him; and as his eyes fell on the young girl his features brightened, and soon wore a happy expression, as if he experienced a great joy.

"You?" he asked, with pleased surprise. "You, maiden, still here! It must be nearly dawn? I slept well till just now. But then at the last— Oh, it was fearful!—Adventus!"

Melissa, however, interrupted this cry, exhorting the emperor to be quiet by putting her finger to her lips; and he understood her and willingly obeyed, especially as she had guessed what he required from the chamberlain, Adventus. She handed him the cloth that lay on the table for him to wipe his streaming forehead. She then brought him drink, and after Caracalla had sat up refreshed, and felt that the pain, which, after a sharp attack, lasted sometimes for days, had now already left him, he said, quite gently, mindful of her sign:

"How much better I feel already; and for this I thank you, Roxana; yes, you know. I like to feel like Alexander, but usually—It is certainly a pleasant thing to be ruler of the universe, for if we wish to punish or reward, no one can limit us. You, child, shall learn that it is Caesar whom you have laid under such obligations. Ask what you will, and I will grant it you."

She whispered eagerly to him:

"Release my father and brother."

"Always the same thing," answered Caracalla, peevishly. "Do you know of nothing better to wish for?"

"No, my lord, no!" cried Melissa, with importunate warmth. "If you will give me what I most care for—"

"I will, yes, I will," interrupted the emperor in a softer voice; but suddenly shrugging his shoulders, he continued, regretfully: "But you must have patience; for, by the Egyptian's orders, your people have been for some time afloat and at sea."

"No!" the girl assured him. "They are still here. Zminis has shamefully deceived you;" and then she informed him of what she had learned from her brother.

Caracalla, in obedience to a softer impulse, had wished to show himself grateful to Melissa. But her demand displeased him; for the sculptor and his son, the philosopher, were the security that should keep Melissa and the painter attached to him. But though his distrust was so strong, offended dignity and the tormenting sense of being deceived caused him to forget everything else; he flew into a rage, and called loudly the names of Epagathos and Adventus.

His voice, quavering with fury, awakened the others also out of their sleep; and after he had shortly and severely rebuked them for their laziness, he commissioned Epagathos to give the prefect, Macrinus, immediate orders not to allow the ship on which Heron and Philip were, to leave the harbor; to set the captives at liberty; and to throw Zminis, the Egyptian, into prison, heavily chained.

When the freedman remarked, humbly, that the prefect was not likely to be found, as he had purposed to be present again that night at the exorcisms of the magician, Serapion, Caesar commanded that Macrinus should be called away from the miracle-monger's house, and the orders given him.

"And if I can not find him?" asked Epagathos.

"Then, once more, events will prove how badly I am served," answered the emperor. "In any case you can act the prefect, and see that my orders are carried out."

The freedman left hastily, and Caracalla sank back exhausted on the pillows.

Melissa let him rest a little while; then she approached him, thanked him profusely, and begged him to keep quiet, lest the pain should return and spoil the approaching day.

He then asked the time, and when Philostratus, who had walked to the window, explained that the fifth hour after midnight was past, Caracalla bade him prepare a bath.

The physician sanctioned this wish, and Caesar then gave his hand to the girl, saying, feebly and in a gentle voice: "The pain still keeps away. I should be better if I could moderate my impatience. An early bath often does me good after a bad night. Only go. The sleep that you know so well how to give to others, you scarcely allow to visit you. I only beg that you will be at hand. We shall both, I think, feel strengthened when next I call you."

Melissa then bade him a grateful farewell; but as she was approaching the doorway he called again after her, and asked her with an altered voice, shortly and sternly:

"You will agree with your father if he abuses me?"

"What an idea!" she answered, energetically. "He knows who robbed him of his liberty, and from me shall he learn who has restored it to him."

"Good!" murmured the emperor. "Yet remember this also: I need your assistance and that of your brother's, the painter. If your father attempts to alienate you—"

Here he suddenly let fall his arm, which he had raised threateningly, and continued in a confidential whisper: "But how can I ever show you anything but kindness? Is it not so? You already feel the secret tie— You know? Am I mistaken when I fancy that it grieves you to be separated from me?"

"Certainly not," she replied, gently, and bowed her head.

"Then go," he continued, kindly. "The day will come yet when you will feel that I am as necessary to your soul as you are to mine. But you do not yet know how impatient I can be. I must be able to think of you with pleasure— always with pleasure—always."

Thereupon he nodded to her, and his eyelids remained for some time in spasmodic movement. Philostratus was prepared to accompany the young girl, but Caracalla prevented him by calling:

"Lead me to my bath. If it does me good, as I trust it will, I have many things to talk over with you."

Melissa did not hear the last words. Gladly and quickly she hurried through the empty, dimly lighted rooms, and found Alexander in a sitting position, half asleep and half awake, with closed eyes. Then she drew near to him on tiptoe, and, as his nodding head fell on his breast, she laughed and woke him with a kiss.

The lamps were not yet burned out, and, as he looked into her face with surprise, his also brightened, and jumping up quickly he exclaimed:

"All's well; we have you back again, and you have succeeded! Our father-I see it in your face—and Philip also, are at liberty!"

"Yes, yes, yes," she answered, gladly; "and now we will go together and fetch them ourselves from the harbor."

Alexander raised his eyes and arms to heaven in rapture, and Melissa imitated him; and thus, without words, though with fervent devotion, they with one accord thanked the gods for their merciful ruling.

They then set out together, and Alexander said: "I feel as if nothing but gratitude flowed through all my veins. At any rate, I have learned for the first time what fear is. That evil guest certainly haunts this place. Let us go now. On the way you shall tell me everything."

"Only one moment's patience," she begged, cheerfully, and hurried into the chief priest's rooms. The lady Euryale was still expecting her, and as she kissed her she looked with sincere pleasure into her bright but tearful eyes.

At first she was bent on making Melissa rest; for she would yet require all her strength. But she saw that the girl's wish to go and meet her father was justifiable; she placed her own mantle over her shoulders— for the air was cool before sunrise—and at last accompanied her into the anteroom. Directly the girl had disappeared, she turned to her sister-in-law's slave, who had waited there the whole night by order of his mistress, and desired him to go and report to her what he had learned about Melissa.

The brother and sister met the slave Argutis outside the Serapeum. He had heard at Seleukus's house where his young mistress was staying, and had made friends with the chief priest's servants.

When, late in the evening, he heard that Melissa was still with Caesar, he had become so uneasy that he had waited the whole night through, first on the steps of a staircase, then walking up and down outside the Serapeum. With a light heart he now accompanied the couple as far as the Aspendia quarter of the town, and he then only parted from them in order that he might inform poor old Dido of his good news, and make preparations for the reception of the home-comers.

After that Melissa hurried along, arm in arm with her brother, through the quiet streets.

Youth, to whom the present belongs entirely, only cares to know the bright side of the future; and even Melissa in her joy at being able to restore liberty to her beloved relations, hardly thought at all of the fact that, when this was done and Caesar should send for her again, there would be new dangers to surmount.

Delighted with her grand success, she first told her brother what her experiences had been with the suffering emperor. Then she started on the recollections of her visit to her lover, and when Alexander opened his heart to her and assured her with fiery ardor that he would not rest till he had won the heart of the lovely Christian, Agatha, she gladly allowed him to talk and promised him her assistance. At last they deliberated how the favor of Caesar—who, Melissa assured him, was cruelly misunderstood—was to be won for their father and Philip; and finally they both imagined the surprise of the old man if he should be the first to meet them after being set at liberty.

The way was far, and when they reached the sea, by the Caesareum in the Bruchium, the palatial quarter of the town, the first glimmer of approaching dawn was showing behind the peninsula of Lochias. The sea was rough, and tossed with heavy, oily waves on the Choma that ran out into the sea like a finger, and on the walls of the Timoneum at its point, where Antonius had hidden his disgrace after the battle of Actium.

Alexander stopped by the pillared temple of Poseidon, which stood close on the shore, between the Choma and the theatre, and, looking toward the flat, horseshoe-shaped coast of the opposite island which still lay in darkness, he asked:

"Do you still remember when we went with our mother over to Antirhodos, and how she allowed us to gather shells in the little harbor? If she were alive to-day, what more could we wish for?"

"That the emperor was gone," exclaimed the girl from the depths of her heart; "that Diodoros were well again; that father could use his hands as he used, and that I might stay with him until Diodoros came to fetch me, and then... oh, if only something could happen to the empire that Caesar might go away-far away, to the farthest hyperborean land!"

"That will soon happen now," answered Alexander. "Philostratus says that the Romans will remain at the utmost a week longer."

"So long?" asked Melissa, startled; but Alexander soon pacified her with the assurance that seven days flew speedily by, and when one looked back on them they seemed to shrink into only as many hours.

"But do not," he continued, cheerfully, "look into the future! We will rejoice, for everything is going so well now!"

He stopped here suddenly and gazed anxiously at the sea, which was no longer completely obscured by the vanishing shadows of night. Melissa looked in the direction of his pointing hand, and when he cried with great excitement, "That is no little boat, it is a ship, and a large one, too!" Melissa added, eagerly, "It is already near the Diabathra. It will reach the Alveus Steganus in a moment, and pass the pharos."

"But yonder is the morning star in the heavens, and the fire is still blazing on the tower," interrupted her brother. "Not till it has been extinguished will they open the outside chain. And yet that ship is steering in a northwesterly direction. It certainly comes out of the royal harbor." He then drew his sister on faster, and when, in a few minutes, they reached the harbor gate, he cried out, much relieved:

"Look there! The chain is still across the entrance. I see it clearly."

"And so do I," said Melissa, decidedly; and while her brother knocked at the gate-house of the little harbor, she continued, eagerly:

"No ships dare go out before sunrise, on account of the rocks—Epagathos said so just now—and that one near the pharos—"

But there was no time to put her thoughts into words; for the broad harbor gate was thrown noisily open, and a troop of Roman soldiers streamed out, followed by several Alexandrian men-at-arms. After them came a prisoner loaded with chains, with whom a leading Roman in warrior's dress was conversing. Both were tall and haggard, and when they approached the brother and sister they recognized in them Macrinus the praetorian prefect, while the prisoner was Zminis the informer.

But the Egyptian also noticed the artist and his companion. His eyes sparkled brightly, and with triumphant scorn he pointed out to sea.

The magician Serapion had persuaded the prefect to let the Egyptian go free. Nothing was yet known in the harbor of Zminis's disgrace, and he had been promptly obeyed as usual, when, spurred on by the magician and his old hatred, he gave the order for the galley which carried the sculptor and his son on board to weigh anchor in spite of the early hour.

Heron and Philip, with chains on their feet, were now rowing on the same bench with the worst criminals; and the old artist's two remaining children stood gazing after the ship that carried away their father and brother into the distance. Melissa stood mute, with tearful eyes, while Alexander, quite beside himself, tried to relieve his rage and grief by empty threats.

Soon, however, his sister's remonstrances caused him to restrain himself, and make inquiry as to whether Macrinus, in obedience to the emperor's orders, had sent a State ship after the galley.

This had been done, and comforted, though sadly disappointed, they started on their way home.

The sun in the mean time had risen, and the streets were filling with people.

They met the old sculptor Lysander, who had been a friend of their father's, outside the magnificent pile of buildings of the Caesareum. The old man took a deep interest in Heron's fate; and, when Alexander asked him modestly what he was doing at that early hour, he pointed to the interior of the building, where the statues of the emperors and empresses stood in a wide circle surrounding a large court-yard, and invited them to come in with him. He had not been able to complete his work—a marble statue of Julia Domna, Caracalla's mother—before the arrival of the emperor. It had been placed here yesterday evening. He had come to see how it looked in its new position.

Melissa had often seen the portrait of Julia on coins and in various pictures, but to-day she was far more strongly attracted than she had ever been before to look in the face of the mother of the man who had so powerfully influenced her own existence and that of her people.

The old master had seen Julia many years ago in her own home at Emesa, as the daughter of Bassianus the high-priest of the Sun in that town; and later, after she had become empress, he had been commanded to take her portrait for her husband, Septimus Severus. While Melissa gazed on the countenance of the beautiful statue, the old artist related how Caracalla's mother had in her youth won all hearts by her wealth of intellect, and the extraordinary knowledge which she had easily acquired and continually added to, through intercourse with learned men. They learned from him that his heart had not remained undisturbed by the charms of his royal model, and Melissa became more and more absorbed in her contemplation of this beautiful work of art.

Lysander had represented the imperial widow standing in flowing draperies, which fell to her feet. She held her charming, youthful head bent slightly on one side, and her right hand held aside the veil which covered the back of her head and fell lightly on her shoulders, a little open over the throat. Her face looked out from under it as if she were listening to a fine song or an interesting speech. Her thick, slightly waving hair framed the lovely oval of her face under the veil, and Alexander agreed with his sister when she expressed the wish that she might but once see this rarely beautiful creature. But the sculptor assured them that they would be disappointed, for time had treated her cruelly.

"I have shown her," he continued, "as she charmed me a generation ago. What you see standing before you is the young girl Julia; I was not capable of representing her as matron or mother. The thought of her son would have spoiled everything,"

"He is capable of better emotions," Alexander declared.

"May be," answered the old man—" I do not know them. May your father and brother be restored to you soon!—I must get to work!"

———————————

Milton Keynes UK
Ingram Content Group UK Ltd.
UKHW031049120324
439302UK00006B/445

9 789357 946032